The Symbiote Chronicles

The Symbiote Chronicles

Matthew Petchinsky

The Symbiote Chronicles: Doctor Who's Venomous Journey
By: Matthew Petchinsky

Disclaimer:
This is a fan-made work inspired by *Doctor Who* and the concept of symbiotes. It is not affiliated with, endorsed by, or connected to the BBC, Marvel Entertainment, Sony Pictures, or any official license holders of *Doctor Who*, Venom, or related properties. All references to characters, concepts, and universes are used in a transformative, creative manner for non-commercial storytelling purposes under fair use. This book is intended as a tribute by fans, for fans.

Introduction

In the vast tapestry of space and time, where stars are born and civilizations crumble, the Doctor has always stood as a sentinel of hope, an enigmatic figure traveling the cosmos in a battered blue box. Known to some as a savior and to others as a harbinger of chaos, the Doctor has faced countless challenges, from ancient gods to sentient machines. Yet, even for someone who has seen the end of the universe and lived to tell the tale, the next adventure promises to be one of the most perplexing and dangerous yet.

This time, the TARDIS takes the Doctor to a seemingly insignificant corner of the galaxy, a small, uncharted planet nestled near the edges of a dying star. The world, though barren at first glance, hums with an eerie energy. Its surface glimmers under the pale light of its sun, as if coated in liquid starlight. But the Doctor quickly discovers this is no ordinary substance. It moves, it reacts, it *thinks*. This alien material, neither fully liquid nor solid, defies the laws of physics and possesses a consciousness of its own—an intelligence both curious and insidious.

The Doctor's initial curiosity turns to alarm as he observes the substance assimilating its surroundings, transforming inert matter into something alive. It mimics life but operates with motives that remain opaque. The Doctor must unravel its origins and intent, navigating a labyrinth of ethical dilemmas. Is it a lifeform seeking companionship? Or is it a predator preparing to consume everything it touches?

As the Doctor delves deeper, aided and hindered by a host of colorful characters, the stakes become increasingly personal. The alien substance begins to interact with the Doctor in ways that suggest it knows more about the Time Lord than it should. It dredges up memories, fears, and choices long buried, forcing the Doctor to confront the weight of centuries of decision-making. In this strange encounter, the boundary between ally and adversary blurs, and the Doctor must grapple with questions that go beyond science and logic—questions of identity, morality, and the very nature of life itself.

Through twists and turns, the Doctor's newest journey challenges their intellect, compassion, and courage like never before. With the fate of entire worlds hanging in the balance, the Doctor must rely on wits, allies, and the indomitable spirit that has carried them through so many adventures. But this time, the stakes are unlike anything they've faced: not just the survival of others, but the survival of their own sense of self.

Join the Doctor in this mesmerizing tale of discovery and danger, where every answer leads to another question, and the unknown lurks in the spaces between. As always, the Doctor must ask: How far would you go to understand the universe? And at what cost?

Chapter 1: Crash on Planet Klyntar

The TARDIS groaned and shuddered violently, its ancient mechanisms protesting under the strain of an unknown force. The Doctor gripped the console tightly, his face alight with a mixture of curiosity and alarm.

"What are you doing, old girl?" he muttered, stroking the console gently with one hand while the other twisted knobs and pushed buttons. "You've flown through supernovas and temporal whirlpools without so much as a hiccup, and now you're behaving like you've got a belly full of bad tea!"

The TARDIS emitted a low, ominous hum in response, and a blaring alarm rang out from the central column.

"Pulled off course? Impossible. I set the coordinates myself—precision work! We were going to the Elysian Fields of Galadros! Lovely this time of year, brilliant sunsets. Unless..." The Doctor's voice trailed off, his expression darkening. "Unless something's pulling *us*."

The central monitor flickered to life, displaying a swirling vortex of shadowy tendrils reaching out from a distant planet. It was a sight that filled the room with an eerie, otherworldly glow. The Doctor's eyes narrowed.

"Klyntar," he said softly, as if the name itself carried weight. "That's new. And very, very ominous."

With a final lurch, the TARDIS plunged into the planet's atmosphere, sending the Doctor sprawling to the floor.

The TARDIS landed with a bone-jarring thud, and for a moment, all was still. The Doctor pulled himself up, dusted off his coat, and glanced around the console room.

"Right then, Klyntar," he said aloud, straightening his bowtie. "Let's see what all the fuss is about."

He grabbed his sonic screwdriver and strode toward the door, hesitating just long enough to mutter, "Hopefully it's not carnivorous fuss."

The air outside was thick and humid, carrying a faint, metallic tang that made the Doctor wrinkle his nose. The ground beneath his feet was a strange amalgamation of black and silver, like molten metal frozen mid-flow. The landscape stretched out in undulating waves, punctuated by jagged spires that gleamed dully in the weak light of the planet's twin moons.

"Hostile-looking," the Doctor remarked, tapping his sonic screwdriver against his palm. "Very uninviting. I like it!"

A low growl echoed in the distance, causing the Doctor to pause. He turned slowly, scanning the horizon. The growl came again, louder this time, and was followed by a chorus of answering snarls.

"Not so inviting," he amended. "And definitely carnivorous fuss."

Suddenly, a flicker of movement caught his eye. A shimmering, liquid-like form slithered out from behind one of the spires, its surface reflecting the dim light like polished obsidian. It moved with an almost predatory grace, and as it drew closer, the Doctor could make out its unsettlingly humanoid shape.

"Ah," he said, stepping back cautiously. "A symbiote, if I'm not mistaken. Lovely to meet you! I'm the Doctor. And you are?"

The creature hissed, its voice a guttural, multi-tonal chorus. *"Intruder. You do not belong."*

"Oh, I get that a lot," the Doctor replied cheerfully, holding up his hands. "Bit of a tourist, me. Just passing through. No need to be hostile."

The symbiote's form shifted, elongating and rippling as it advanced. *"You are not welcome. Leave, or face annihilation."*

"Annihilation? That's a bit extreme, don't you think?" The Doctor's tone was light, but his grip tightened on the sonic screwdriver. "Now, I'm sure we can work this out. Tell me, what's got you so riled up?"

Before the symbiote could respond, a deafening roar split the air. The ground trembled, and the Doctor barely managed to keep his footing as a massive, insect-like creature burst into view. Its exoskeleton was scarred and battered, and its multifaceted eyes glinted with malevolence. The symbiote turned its attention to the newcomer, hissing furiously.

"Enemy! The war is eternal."

The Doctor's eyebrows shot up. "Ah, an ancient feud! That explains the hostility. Well, not entirely, but it's a start."

The insectoid charged, its mandibles snapping, and the symbiote launched itself forward to meet the attack. The two clashed with a force that sent shockwaves rippling through the ground. Black tendrils wrapped around the insectoid's limbs, while the creature's claws tore through the symbiote's shimmering form. It was a battle of sheer ferocity, and the Doctor watched, equal parts horrified and fascinated.

"Right," he said, edging backward. "Time to go."

But before he could retreat, another symbiote appeared, slithering toward him with alarming speed.

"You brought this upon us," it snarled. *"You will pay the price."*

"Now, hold on!" the Doctor protested, raising the sonic screwdriver defensively. "I didn't bring anything! I'm just here to... observe. Mediate, even! Peaceful resolutions are sort of my thing."

The symbiote lunged, and the Doctor dove out of the way, rolling to his feet with surprising agility.

"Or running away," he muttered. "Running away is also my thing."

He bolted toward the TARDIS, the symbiote hot on his heels. The battle between the first symbiote and the insectoid raged on, the air thick with the sounds of snarls, roars, and tearing flesh. As the Doctor reached the TARDIS, he glanced back, his expression grim.

"Ancient war, symbiotes, and hostile locals," he said, yanking open the door. "Brilliant. Just another Tuesday."

The TARDIS door slammed shut behind him, and the Doctor leaned against it, catching his breath. The central console hummed softly, as if in sympathy.

"Well, old girl," he said, straightening up. "Looks like we've got a mystery to solve. And judging by that welcome party, it's going to be a tricky one."

He flipped a switch, and the TARDIS monitor lit up, displaying a holographic map of the planet.

"Klyntar," he murmured, studying the map intently. "Home of the symbiotes, embroiled in an endless war. But why? And what dragged us here in the first place?"

As the TARDIS hummed in response, the Doctor's eyes gleamed with determination.

"Right then," he said, pulling on his coat. "Let's go find some answers."

Chapter 2: A Symbiotic Encounter

The TARDIS doors creaked open, and the Doctor stepped out into the hostile terrain of Klyntar once again. His sonic screwdriver was clutched tightly in one hand, its tip glowing faintly. The holographic map displayed earlier had pinpointed an area rich with unusual energy signatures—just the sort of thing that screamed trouble, and therefore, irresistibly intriguing.

"Right then," he muttered, scanning the horizon. "Rescue mission first, existential crisis later. Classic Doctor priorities."

The symbiote battle from earlier had subsided, but the ground bore scars of the skirmish. Pools of black ichor shimmered ominously in the dim light, pulsing with faint energy. The Doctor tread carefully, his curiosity piqued but his caution firmly in place.

A faint, plaintive cry echoed in the distance. It was a sound filled with desperation and pain, cutting through the oppressive silence of the planet. The Doctor froze.

"Hello?" he called out, his voice carrying a note of concern. "If you're injured, stay put! Help is on the way!"

The cry came again, weaker this time. The Doctor quickened his pace, weaving between jagged spires and gelatinous pools. He reached a small clearing where a native Klyntarian lay sprawled, its humanoid form flickering with faint bioluminescence. Thick, obsidian tendrils bound its limbs, anchoring it to the ground.

"Oh, you poor thing," the Doctor murmured, kneeling beside the creature. "Looks like someone doesn't play fair around here."

The native's eyes, like molten silver, flickered open. "Run... before it comes back," it rasped.

"Run? Not my style," the Doctor said with a reassuring smile, brandishing his sonic screwdriver. "Let's see about freeing you, shall we?"

The sonic emitted a series of high-pitched whirs as the Doctor aimed it at the tendrils. They hissed and writhed but didn't release their hold.

"Stubborn, aren't you?" he muttered, adjusting the frequency. "Don't worry; I'm very good at stubborn."

As the tendrils began to loosen, a shadow fell over them. The Doctor glanced up and froze. A towering mass of shifting black material loomed above, its surface rippling with energy. Two piercing white eyes emerged from the void, and a deep, guttural voice echoed.

"*Foolish Time Lord,*" it rumbled. "*You meddle in matters beyond your comprehension.*"

"Ah, you must be the local enforcer," the Doctor said, standing and slipping the screwdriver into his pocket. "Lovely to meet you. I'd offer tea, but I suspect you're not the type."

The entity didn't respond with words. Instead, it lunged. Tendrils shot out, wrapping around the Doctor with lightning speed. He struggled, but the strength of the entity was overwhelming.

"Now, hold on!" the Doctor protested. "This is a bit forward, don't you think?"

The tendrils pulsed, and a sharp, alien sensation flooded the Doctor's mind—a melding of two consciousnesses. His vision blurred, and for a brief moment, the world dissolved into a chaotic swirl of black and white. When clarity returned, he was on his knees, gasping for breath.

"*Interesting,*" a voice echoed in his mind. It was dark and smooth, with a hint of curiosity. "*Your mind is... complex. And your body... fascinating.*"

The Doctor groaned, pushing himself upright. "What... what are you?"

"I am Venom," the voice replied, its tone laced with both pride and menace. "And now, Doctor, we are one."

The Doctor staggered to his feet, his body feeling strangely heavy and yet unnervingly strong. "Oh no, no, no, no. This won't do at all," he said, waving his hands—hands that were now partially covered in black, shimmering material. "Symbiotic relationships aren't my thing. Bit too clingy."

Venom chuckled. "*You have no choice. I have seen your potential—your intelligence, your regeneration. Together, we could be unstoppable.*"

"Unstoppable? Don't need to be. Stoppable's worked just fine for me so far," the Doctor quipped, though his voice was tinged with unease.

The native Klyntarian, now free from its bonds, watched in horror. "You must resist it," it said weakly. "If it bonds fully, it will corrupt you."

"Corrupt? Me?" The Doctor shook his head. "I'm incorruptible. Mostly. Well, on good days. Venom, we need to have a chat about boundaries."

"*We have no time for that,*" Venom growled. "*Enemies approach.*"

The ground trembled, and a horde of insectoid creatures emerged from the shadows. Their mandibles clicked in unison, a sound that sent shivers down the Doctor's spine.

"Ah, reinforcements," he muttered. "That's never a good sign."

Venom's influence surged, and the Doctor felt an uncontrollable urge to fight. His hands transformed into claws, black tendrils lashing out toward the attackers with precision and power.

"No, no, no!" the Doctor shouted, struggling to regain control. "I don't *do* claws! Fighting isn't my style!"

"*It is now,*" Venom replied, relishing the chaos.

Despite his protests, the Doctor's actions were swift and brutal. The insectoids fell one by one, their shattered forms littering the battlefield. When the last of them fled, the Doctor collapsed to his knees, his body trembling.

"This... this isn't me," he whispered, his voice hollow.

"*It is survival,*" Venom said simply. "*And you will learn to embrace it.*"

The native Klyntarian approached cautiously. "Doctor, you must find a way to separate. The symbiote will consume you."

The Doctor looked up, his eyes a mix of defiance and fear. "Don't worry. I've faced worse than this. I'll find a way. Always do."

But as Venom's laughter echoed in his mind, the Doctor couldn't shake the chilling realization that this might be one battle he couldn't win alone.

Chapter 3: The Hungry Shadow

The Doctor stumbled back into the TARDIS, slamming the door shut behind him. He was breathing heavily, his body trembling as he leaned against the cool, reassuring surface of the ancient wooden frame. The soft hum of the TARDIS filled the room, a stark contrast to the chaos he'd just escaped.

"Right, safe for now," he muttered, wiping sweat from his brow. "Well, mostly safe."

"*Safe?*" Venom's voice resonated in his mind, deep and sardonic. "*You are never safe. Not with me.*"

The Doctor winced, clutching his temples. "You're not supposed to be here! My mind, my rules!"

"*Your body is fascinating,*" Venom continued, ignoring the Doctor's protest. "*You are not like the others I've bonded with. Your energy... it's endless. Ancient. I want more.*"

"That's regeneration energy you're sniffing about," the Doctor snapped, pacing the console room. "It's not something to toy with. Or, I should say, *I'm* not something to toy with!"

The TARDIS lights flickered, responding to the tension between its pilot and the invasive entity. Venom seemed unimpressed.

"*Regeneration. A concept unique to your kind. You are a Time Lord, a species built on resilience and reinvention. But even you have limits.*"

The Doctor paused, narrowing his eyes. "And you think you've figured me out, have you? That you can just siphon off a piece of me like I'm a particularly tasty snack?"

Venom didn't answer immediately. Instead, a strange sensation spread through the Doctor's body. His chest felt tight, his hearts pounding erratically. He gasped, stumbling toward the console, gripping its edge for support.

"*Yes,*" Venom finally replied, his voice smoother now, almost smug. "*I don't need all of it. Just a taste. Let me show you.*"

Before the Doctor could respond, a surge of energy coursed through him. His body lit up with golden, crackling light—the unmistakable glow of regeneration energy. It felt like fire and euphoria all at once, burning through him and yet filling him with an intoxicating power.

"No!" the Doctor shouted, struggling against the sensation. "Stop it! You don't know what you're messing with!"

"*Oh, I know exactly what I'm doing,*" Venom purred, his voice a sinister whisper in the Doctor's ear. "*This power is extraordinary. It makes us stronger.*"

The Doctor dropped to his knees, his body glowing as if caught mid-regeneration. He gritted his teeth, wrestling for control. "This isn't strength—it's theft! You can't just take it! You'll—"

The golden light dimmed abruptly, leaving the Doctor slumped on the floor, panting. Venom's influence receded slightly, though his presence remained like a shadow lingering just out of reach.

"*Impressive,*" Venom said. "*You survived. Most would not.*"

"Survived? You nearly burned me out!" the Doctor snapped, forcing himself upright. "Regeneration energy isn't infinite, you know. Every drop of it is precious."

"*And yet, you waste it on sentimentality,*" Venom countered. "*You have lived for centuries, and yet you hesitate. You fear your own power.*"

The Doctor's expression darkened. "Power isn't about domination, Venom. It's about responsibility. Something you clearly lack."

"*Responsibility?*" Venom sneered. "*You play at being a god, meddling in the lives of lesser beings. Don't speak to me of responsibility.*"

"That's rich, coming from an alien parasite!" the Doctor shot back. "You think you're superior because you can hijack someone's body? Let me tell you something: you're not the first entity to think it could control me, and you certainly won't be the last."

Venom fell silent, as if considering the Doctor's words. The TARDIS, sensing the Doctor's distress, dimmed its lights further, casting the room in a somber glow. The console hummed softly, a gentle reminder of the bond between the Doctor and his ship.

Finally, Venom spoke again, his tone more measured. *"You are... unusual. A being of intellect and emotion. I have never encountered anything quite like you."*

"That's because there's no one else like me," the Doctor replied, standing fully now, his voice regaining its usual confidence. "And if you think I'm going to let you use me as some kind of battery, you've got another thing coming."

"I could leave," Venom said, almost mockingly. *"But would you survive? The bond is... complicated. We are entwined now, Doctor. You need me as much as I need you."*

"Do I?" The Doctor raised an eyebrow, tapping his chin thoughtfully. "Or is that just another trick to keep me compliant? Oh, you're good, I'll give you that. But I'm better."

"You think you can defeat me?" Venom asked, his voice filled with both amusement and menace.

"Defeat you?" The Doctor grinned. "Oh, no, Venom. I don't defeat enemies. I outsmart them. And I'm afraid you've chosen the wrong Time Lord to tangle with."

Venom didn't respond immediately, but the Doctor could feel his presence shift—less aggressive, more contemplative. It was as if Venom was weighing his options, trying to understand the mind of his host.

For now, the Doctor knew, it was a stalemate. But he also knew that the longer Venom remained bonded to him, the greater the danger. Venom was curious, intelligent, and hungry for power. And the Doctor, for all his resilience, was not invincible.

"We shall see, Doctor," Venom said finally. *"For now, we are allies. But do not forget—I am always watching."*

The Doctor sighed, brushing off his coat. "Trust me, Venom, I never forget."

He turned to the TARDIS console, his fingers dancing over the controls. "Let's find out what's really going on here. And if you behave yourself, I might even let you tag along. Just... no more stealing my energy, all right?"

"*For now,*" Venom replied, his voice echoing faintly in the Doctor's mind.

The Doctor smirked. "That's the spirit. Now, let's solve this mystery, shall we?"

As the TARDIS hummed and whirred to life, the Doctor couldn't shake the feeling that this was only the beginning of a much larger, more dangerous journey. And for once, he wasn't entirely sure if he'd be able to come out unscathed.

Chapter 4: A Symbiote's Curiosity

The TARDIS hummed softly as the Doctor paced around the console, muttering to himself and occasionally glancing at the readouts. Despite the chaos of recent events, his mind was a whirlwind of theories and strategies. Yet, he couldn't shake the sensation of being watched—because he *was*.

"*Your ship...*" Venom's voice echoed in his mind, smooth and contemplative. "*It is alive.*"

"Of course, she is," the Doctor replied, not missing a beat as he adjusted a lever. "The TARDIS is more than just a ship. She's my home, my companion. Well, *one* of my companions. And far too clever for you to get your tendrils into, so don't even think about it."

"*Fascinating,*" Venom mused. "*A machine with consciousness. But it is bound to you. Like I am now.*"

"Oh, there's nothing *like* you, Venom," the Doctor said with a raised eyebrow. "You're a bit of a unique problem. Well, not entirely unique—let's not forget the time I dealt with sentient nanobots. Or the psychic leeches of Archavia. Still, you're in a league of your own."

"*I sense vast energy within this ship,*" Venom continued, ignoring the Doctor's quip. "*It bends the rules of the universe. Time. Space. It is intoxicating.*"

The Doctor froze mid-step, his face darkening. "You keep your slimy mitts off her, understood? You've already taken liberties with my biology—try anything with the TARDIS, and you'll regret it."

"*Relax, Time Lord,*" Venom replied with an amused tone. "*I am... curious. Nothing more.*"

The Doctor sighed, running a hand through his hair. "Curiosity, Venom, can be dangerous. But I'll admit, it's better than outright destruction. So, since we're sharing headspace, how about a bit of a learning opportunity?"

"*Explain,*" Venom said, intrigued.

The Doctor grinned, flipping a switch on the console. "How about I show you what the TARDIS can really do?"

At that moment, a sharp, rhythmic beeping interrupted their conversation. The Doctor's expression shifted, the playful glint in his eyes replaced with concern.

"Distress signal," he said, his fingers flying across the controls. "Faint, but definitely urgent."

"*A cry for help,*" Venom observed. "*You cannot resist these.*"

"Of course not," the Doctor replied. "If someone's in trouble, we answer. That's how this works. It's what I do."

"*Why?*" Venom asked, genuinely curious. "*What do you gain from this?*"

"It's not about gaining, Venom," the Doctor said, pausing to meet the symbiote's unseen gaze. "It's about doing the right thing. Helping people. Standing up when no one else will."

Venom was silent for a moment, then said, "*You are... strange. But intriguing.*"

The Doctor smiled faintly, pulling a lever. "Hang on, Venom. We're going to see where this distress call leads."

The TARDIS materialized with its usual groaning wheeze, settling on the surface of a barren, crimson-tinged planet. The Doctor stepped out cautiously, his eyes scanning the desolate landscape.

The air was thin but breathable, and the ground beneath his boots was cracked and dry, as if the planet had been drained of life. In the distance, jagged mountains loomed, their peaks shrouded in swirling red clouds.

"Lovely spot," the Doctor said sarcastically. "Perfect for a picnic. Assuming you like your sandwiches with a side of existential dread."

"*I feel... something,*" Venom murmured, his voice quieter now. "*This place is wrong.*"

"Perceptive of you," the Doctor replied, his tone clipped. "Something terrible happened here, no doubt about it."

Following the faint signal on his sonic screwdriver, the Doctor made his way across the cracked ground. The closer he got, the more oppressive the atmosphere became. Finally, he came upon the source of the signal—a downed starship, its hull scorched and riddled with holes.

The Doctor knelt beside the wreckage, scanning it with the sonic screwdriver. "Crash happened recently. Minimal survivors, if any."

"*Someone is here,*" Venom said, his tone sharp. "*I can feel them.*"

The Doctor straightened, glancing around. "Where?"

Before Venom could respond, a faint voice called out. "Help... please..."

The Doctor turned, spotting a figure slumped against a rock. He hurried over, his hearts sinking at the sight. The survivor, a humanoid with pale blue skin and faintly glowing eyes, was gravely injured. Their breathing was shallow, their body covered in burns.

"It's all right," the Doctor said gently, kneeling beside them. "You're safe now. I'm the Doctor."

The figure's eyes fluttered open. "Doctor... the shadows... they came from the shadows..."

"Shadows?" the Doctor repeated, frowning. "What shadows?"

But before the survivor could answer, their eyes widened in fear. "It's here..."

A chill ran down the Doctor's spine as he turned, just in time to see a massive, writhing shadow detach itself from the wreckage. The creature, a twisted mass of dark tendrils, radiated malevolence as it loomed toward them.

"*A predator,*" Venom hissed, his voice tinged with both fear and anger. "*It feeds on the weak.*"

The Doctor stood protectively in front of the survivor. "Not on my watch," he said, raising the sonic screwdriver. "Let's see how you like a burst of sonic frequencies, shall we?"

The shadow creature recoiled as the sonic emitted a piercing whine, but it didn't retreat. Instead, it grew larger, its tendrils lashing out with alarming speed.

"*You are no match for it!*" Venom warned. "*Let me take control!*"

"No!" the Doctor shouted, dodging a tendril. "I don't fight like that!"

"*Then you will die!*" Venom snarled. "*And so will they!*"

The Doctor hesitated, his mind racing. He hated violence, but Venom was right—this was a battle he couldn't win alone.

"Fine," he muttered. "But I'm in charge, understood?"

"*Agreed,*" Venom said, his voice filled with a dark excitement.

The Doctor felt the symbiote surge through his body, black tendrils wrapping around him as his form shifted. His hands transformed into claws, his reflexes sharpened, and his strength multiplied. Together, they faced the shadow creature, their movements fluid and deadly.

The battle was fierce, the Doctor and Venom fighting as one. Tendrils clashed against tendrils, and with a final, powerful strike, the shadow creature dissolved into a wisp of darkness.

As the dust settled, the Doctor stumbled back, the symbiote receding. He dropped to his knees, breathing heavily.

"*You survived because of me,*" Venom said, his tone smug.

The Doctor didn't respond immediately, his gaze fixed on the injured survivor. Finally, he whispered, "At what cost?"

For the first time, Venom was silent.

Chapter 5: Symbiosis in Space

The TARDIS materialized in the middle of a sprawling, domed city that glittered with iridescent lights. Outside the protective dome lay a barren planet ravaged by volcanic eruptions, the air thick with toxic clouds. Inside, however, the city thrived, its citizens—tall, willowy beings with translucent skin that shimmered like opals—hurrying about with an air of quiet urgency.

The Doctor stepped out of the TARDIS, his coat billowing behind him, Venom's presence a constant weight in his mind.

"Now this is more like it," the Doctor said, taking in the stunning cityscape. "Architecture that blends form and function beautifully. Haven't seen something this elegant since the crystal spires of Urathalon. Don't suppose you're a fan of art, Venom?"

"*Art is irrelevant,*" Venom replied, his tone dismissive. "*Survival is what matters.*"

The Doctor rolled his eyes. "Always the pragmatist, aren't you? You'd be surprised how often beauty and survival go hand in hand."

"*Focus, Time Lord,*" Venom hissed. "*Something is wrong here. I can feel it.*"

The Doctor's expression shifted, his jovial demeanor giving way to a more serious tone. "You're right. Something's off. The air feels... heavy, even in here."

He flipped open his sonic screwdriver, scanning the surroundings. The readings were concerning—energy spikes throughout the city, concentrated toward a central hub. But more worrying was the faint but unmistakable presence of dark energy—similar to Venom's, yet distinctly different.

"Right, we're investigating that," the Doctor declared, pointing toward the hub.

The Doctor weaved through the bustling streets, drawing the occasional curious glance from the citizens. He arrived at the central hub, a towering structure that pulsed with soft blue light. At its base, a group of the translucent beings stood in a heated discussion.

"Excuse me!" the Doctor called, approaching them. "Hello! I'm the Doctor. Mind if I ask what's going on?"

The tallest of the group turned, their opalescent skin shimmering faintly. "You are not one of us," they said, their voice melodic yet tinged with suspicion. "Why are you here?"

"Good question," the Doctor replied, flashing a disarming smile. "Short answer: I'm here to help. Long answer: I followed a distress signal, and it led me to your lovely city. Now, I can't help but notice that you seem... agitated. Care to fill me in?"

The being hesitated, then gestured toward the pulsing tower. "The Core is failing. It powers our city and shields us from the planet's toxic environment. If it collapses, we will not survive."

The Doctor frowned, scanning the Core with his sonic screwdriver. The readings were chaotic, the energy destabilized and flickering dangerously.

"What's causing the instability?" he asked, already piecing together possibilities.

"We suspect an invader," the being replied. "A predator. It arrived weeks ago, and since then, our systems have been failing one by one."

"*It sounds like one of my kind,*" Venom remarked, his voice low and contemplative. "*A rogue symbiote.*"

The Doctor stiffened. "If it is, then we've got a problem. A big one."

"*This is an opportunity,*" Venom said, his tone shifting. "*We could absorb it. Its strength would become ours.*"

The Doctor's expression darkened. "We're not absorbing anything, Venom. We're here to *help*, not feed."

"*Helping them could mean sacrificing us,*" Venom countered. "*Would you risk yourself for them?*"

"Every single time," the Doctor replied firmly. "That's what being the Doctor means."

The Doctor made his way into the Core chamber, the air thick with static energy. The Core itself, a massive crystalline structure, pulsed erratically, its light dimming and flaring in chaotic bursts. Tendrils of dark, viscous material clung to its base, pulsating with malevolent energy.

"There it is," the Doctor muttered. "Your rogue symbiote. And it's feeding off the Core."

"*It grows stronger with each second,*" Venom observed. "*We must destroy it.*"

"No," the Doctor said, pulling out his sonic screwdriver. "We'll sever its connection to the Core and find a way to contain it."

"*Contain? Foolish,*" Venom growled. "*It will destroy you the moment it escapes.*"

"Not if I stop it first," the Doctor replied, his voice steady but tense.

The symbiote noticed their presence, its tendrils writhing as it turned toward them. Its form was massive, a twisted amalgamation of liquid and shadow, its glowing white eyes filled with malice.

"*Time Lord... and kin,*" it hissed. "*You should not have come.*"

The Doctor stepped forward, holding the sonic screwdriver aloft. "Funny, I hear that a lot. Listen, you've caused enough damage here. Let's talk this out before things get messy, shall we?"

The rogue symbiote roared, its tendrils lashing out. Venom surged through the Doctor's body instinctively, black armor forming around him as claws extended from his hands.

"*We end this now,*" Venom snarled.

"No!" the Doctor shouted, struggling to suppress Venom's influence. "We don't kill unless there's no other way!"

"*This creature is beyond redemption,*" Venom growled. "*It will consume everything.*"

The rogue symbiote struck again, and the Doctor narrowly dodged, using the sonic screwdriver to emit a pulse of energy that disrupted its tendrils. The Core flickered, stabilizing slightly as the rogue symbiote recoiled.

"See? We don't need to kill it," the Doctor said, panting. "Just need to outsmart it."

"*You risk everything for nothing,*" Venom snapped. "*Your principles will get you killed.*"

"They're what keep me alive," the Doctor replied. "Now, trust me. Let me do this my way."

With a final surge of effort, the Doctor used the sonic screwdriver to overload the Core's protective systems, emitting a burst of energy that severed the rogue symbiote's connection. The creature shrieked, its form dissipating into the air like smoke.

The Doctor collapsed to his knees, breathing heavily as Venom receded.

"*You were reckless,*" Venom said after a long pause. "*But effective.*"

The Doctor managed a weak smile. "That's the job description. Now, let's get out of here before something else decides to attack."

As the TARDIS dematerialized, the Doctor couldn't shake the weight of Venom's words—or the gnawing fear that his principles might not always be enough to keep the darkness at bay.

Chapter 6: Symbiotes Unleashed

The TARDIS shuddered violently as it hurtled through the Time Vortex, the central console sparking as warning lights flared. The Doctor frantically twisted knobs and flipped levers, his face a mask of determination.

"Not good, not good at all," he muttered, glancing at the monitor. "Rogue symbiotes hitching a ride through the Vortex? That's a first."

"*They are persistent,*" Venom remarked, his voice cold and calculating. "*They sense the power of your home world.*"

The Doctor's hand froze mid-motion. "Gallifrey," he said quietly, his voice heavy with dread. "They're after the Time Lords."

"*Your people are strong. They will make ideal hosts,*" Venom said, almost admiringly.

The Doctor slammed a lever with uncharacteristic fury. "Not on my watch. Gallifrey has suffered enough, and I'll be damned if I let you or anyone else use it as a playground."

The TARDIS jolted to a sudden halt, the familiar *vworp-vworp* of its engines fading. The Doctor steadied himself against the console, his expression grim.

"Right," he said, adjusting his coat. "If we're doing this, we're doing it fast."

"*And if you fail?*" Venom asked, his voice a low, dangerous whisper.

"I don't fail," the Doctor shot back. "Not today."

The Doctor stepped out into the warm, golden light of Gallifrey's twin suns. The familiar sight of the Capitol's towering spires brought a brief wave of nostalgia, but it was quickly overshadowed by the chaos unfolding before him.

Time Lords and citizens alike ran in panic as dark, writhing symbiotes lashed out, their oily forms latching onto anyone within reach. The creatures moved with terrifying speed, their tendrils snaking around necks and limbs as they sought to bond with new hosts.

"No, no, no," the Doctor muttered, his hearts sinking. "This is worse than I thought."

"*Beautiful,*" Venom hissed. "*They spread quickly. Efficient predators.*"

"They're not predators—they're parasites!" the Doctor snapped. "And they'll destroy everything if we don't stop them."

"*You mean if you don't stop them,*" Venom corrected. "*You're the one who refuses to embrace their strength.*"

The Doctor ignored him, racing toward the Capitol. Inside, he found the High Council chamber in disarray. Time Lords in their ceremonial robes stood in clusters, their normally calm demeanor replaced by panic. President Rassilon stood at the center, his expression one of barely controlled rage.

"Doctor!" Rassilon barked as soon as he saw him. "What is the meaning of this invasion? Did you bring them here?"

"Oh, wonderful," the Doctor said, throwing up his hands. "Gallifrey is under attack, and the first thing you do is blame me. Typical."

"You've brought chaos to our doorstep before," Rassilon snarled, stepping closer. "Can you deny it this time?"

"Yes, actually," the Doctor said, pointing a finger at him. "This wasn't me. This is the result of a faction of rogue symbiotes from Klyntar deciding to hitch a ride through the Time Vortex. And if we don't act quickly, they'll make every Time Lord here their host."

The room fell silent. Finally, one of the Council members, a stern-faced woman, stepped forward. "Doctor, you've faced these creatures before. How do we stop them?"

"Good question," the Doctor said, pacing. "Symbiotes need hosts to survive, but their bond can be severed if you disrupt their connection long enough. The problem is, these aren't just any symbiotes. They're organized. Intelligent. They'll fight back."

"And they are winning," Venom added darkly. *"Your people are no match for them."*

The Doctor froze. "You're wrong," he said quietly. "Gallifrey isn't defenseless. We have the Matrix, temporal shields, and—"

A deafening roar interrupted him. The chamber doors burst open as a massive symbiote, larger and more grotesque than the others, stormed in. Its tendrils lashed out, knocking over Time Lords and tearing through the ornate walls.

"The leader," Venom whispered, almost in awe. *"Impressive."*

"Not the word I'd use," the Doctor muttered, pulling out his sonic screwdriver. "Everyone, get back!"

He activated the sonic, aiming it at the creature. The device emitted a high-pitched whine, causing the symbiote to writhe and shriek, but it didn't retreat. Instead, it surged forward, its tendrils aiming for Rassilon.

"Watch out!" the Doctor yelled, diving in front of the President. The tendrils wrapped around him instead, and he felt the cold, invasive presence of the symbiote pushing into his mind.

"Doctor!" Rassilon shouted, but the Doctor raised a hand, his face strained.

"I'm fine," he managed, though his voice was shaky. "Just... give me a moment."

Inside his mind, the Doctor felt the symbiote leader trying to assert dominance. But it wasn't alone. Venom was there too, snarling and fighting back.

"This host is mine," Venom growled, his voice filled with fury. *"You will not take him."*

The Doctor felt the clash of wills, the raw, feral power of the two symbiotes battling for control. He gritted his teeth, forcing his own consciousness to the forefront.

"Both of you, stop!" he shouted. "This is my mind, my body, and I'm not sharing it with either of you!"

The symbiote leader faltered, its tendrils loosening slightly. Venom, sensing an opportunity, surged forward, overwhelming the invader and forcing it to retreat. The Doctor gasped as the connection broke, the symbiote leader retreating with an enraged roar.

"Doctor, are you—" Rassilon began, but the Doctor cut him off.

"No time for questions," he said, standing shakily. "We need to act now. If we don't contain these creatures, Gallifrey is finished."

The Doctor turned to the Matrix interface, a massive, glowing console at the center of the room. He began working furiously, his fingers flying over the controls.

"What are you doing?" the stern-faced Council member asked.

"Creating a containment field," the Doctor replied. "It'll trap the symbiotes and cut them off from their hosts."

"*A bold plan,*" Venom said. "*But what if it fails?*"

"It won't," the Doctor said firmly, though his voice betrayed a hint of doubt.

The symbiote leader roared again, charging toward the Doctor. Rassilon and the others tried to stop it, but it barreled through them effortlessly.

"Doctor, look out!" someone shouted.

The Doctor didn't flinch. At the last second, he slammed the final control, and the Matrix flared to life. A blinding light filled the room as the containment field activated, trapping the symbiotes in a shimmering, golden barrier.

The leader shrieked, its tendrils clawing at the barrier, but it couldn't break through. Slowly, its form dissolved, the energy sustaining it severed.

The Doctor collapsed against the console, breathing heavily. "There," he said weakly. "That should hold them."

For now, Gallifrey was safe. But as the Doctor looked out at the devastated city, he couldn't shake the feeling that this was only the beginning. Venom's presence in his mind remained, a constant reminder of the danger that lurked within—and the darkness he might one day have to confront.

Chapter 7: Venom's Evolution

The TARDIS floated in the vast expanse of space, orbiting a nebula that shimmered with iridescent colors. Inside, the Doctor leaned against the console, his arms crossed, staring at the monitor that displayed diagnostic scans of himself and Venom.

"You're changing," the Doctor said aloud, his voice tinged with curiosity and wariness.

"*I am evolving,*" Venom replied, his tone less aggressive than usual. "*Your energy... it has transformed me.*"

The Doctor turned to face the room, pacing thoughtfully. "Regeneration energy is powerful, yes, but it's not a cure-all. It's not meant to be absorbed by others. You're not just evolving—you're adapting. Becoming... something else."

"*And you fear me for it,*" Venom said, his voice quieter but still sharp. "*You fear that I am becoming stronger than you.*"

"Stronger?" The Doctor shook his head, his voice softening. "No, Venom. What I fear is the unknown. You've already pushed boundaries I'd rather not cross. And now, here you are, growing, changing—and I have no idea what you'll become."

There was a pause before Venom responded. "*Neither do I.*"

The TARDIS interior was silent except for the rhythmic hum of the engines. The Doctor sat on the floor, his back against the console, staring at the ceiling. His mind raced with possibilities, each one more troubling than the last.

"Why are you so quiet?" the Doctor asked finally, breaking the silence. "You're usually much more... vocal."

"*I am thinking,*" Venom said, his voice distant. "*About you. About me. About what we have become.*"

"That's new," the Doctor remarked, raising an eyebrow. "Self-reflection isn't exactly in your wheelhouse."

"*It is now,*" Venom replied. "*Your energy—it is more than physical. It carries your thoughts, your emotions, your... morality. It is changing me.*"

The Doctor's expression softened. "And how does that feel?"

"*Strange,*" Venom admitted. "*I have always been a predator. I consumed to survive, destroyed to thrive. But now, I... question.*"

The Doctor leaned forward, intrigued. "Question what?"

"*My purpose,*" Venom said. "*My instincts. You value life, even when it is weak or insignificant. Why?*"

The Doctor smiled faintly. "Life isn't about strength or significance, Venom. It's about potential. Every life has the capacity to grow, to change, to create. That's what makes it precious."

"*But not all life is good,*" Venom countered. "*Some destroy without purpose. Some kill without reason.*"

"Yes," the Doctor said softly. "But even then, there's the possibility for redemption. For change. I believe in that."

Venom was silent for a moment, as if digesting the words. Finally, he said, "*Your belief... it is affecting me. I feel... compelled to protect now. To preserve. Is this what you call morality?*"

The Doctor chuckled, his gaze thoughtful. "Something like that. Morality's a tricky thing, Venom. It's not black and white—it's shades of grey. But it's what keeps us from losing ourselves."

The TARDIS jolted suddenly, throwing the Doctor off balance. Alarms blared as the central console lit up with red warning lights.

"What now?" the Doctor muttered, leaping to his feet and scanning the monitor. "Ah, a distress beacon. Again."

"*You cannot resist these cries for help,*" Venom remarked.

"Of course not," the Doctor replied, flipping switches. "It's what I do."

The TARDIS materialized in the middle of a battlefield. The Doctor stepped out cautiously, his sonic screwdriver in hand. The air was thick with smoke, and the ground was littered with debris and wounded beings from two warring factions.

"War," the Doctor muttered, his expression darkening. "It's always war."

A cry for help caught his attention, and he raced toward a group of injured civilians trapped beneath rubble. As he began working to free them, Venom's voice echoed in his mind.

"They are weak. Why save them?"

"Because they're innocent," the Doctor snapped. "They didn't ask for this war. They're just trying to survive."

"And the ones who started the war?" Venom asked. *"Do they deserve your mercy?"*

The Doctor hesitated, his hands pausing over the rubble. "That's not for me to decide. My job is to help, not judge."

Venom fell silent, but the Doctor could feel him processing the answer.

Later, as the Doctor worked tirelessly to tend to the wounded, Venom spoke again. This time, his tone was different—softer, almost uncertain.

"Doctor," he said. *"I feel... something. When you save them. When you fight for them. It is... satisfying."*

The Doctor smiled faintly, wiping sweat from his brow. "That's called doing the right thing, Venom. Feels good, doesn't it?"

"Yes," Venom said. *"But it is also... painful. I see their suffering. I feel their fear. It lingers."*

The Doctor nodded. "That's the price of compassion. You feel the weight of their pain, but you also feel the joy of their survival. It's what makes it all worthwhile."

"I do not understand everything," Venom admitted. *"But I want to."*

The Doctor straightened, his smile widening. "That's a start, Venom. And it's a good one."

As the TARDIS left the battlefield behind, the Doctor sat at the console, his expression thoughtful. Venom's presence in his mind was quieter now, less invasive, and more... contemplative.

"You're evolving, Venom," the Doctor said aloud. "Not just physically, but emotionally. Morally. You're becoming something more."

"*Thanks to you,*" Venom said. "*You have shown me another way. A better way.*"

The Doctor's smile was bittersweet. "Maybe. But the real question is, what will you do with that knowledge?"

Venom didn't answer immediately. When he finally spoke, his voice was filled with conviction. "*I will protect. I will preserve. And I will learn.*"

The Doctor leaned back, his hearts lighter than they'd been in days. "Good. That's all I could ever ask."

Chapter 8: The Symbiotic Siege of Gallifrey

The skies above Gallifrey darkened with the swirling mass of rogue symbiotes. Like a tide of liquid darkness, they poured out of the rift in space, their tendrils coiling and snapping as they descended upon the gleaming towers of the Time Lords' Capitol. Alarms blared across the city as Time Lords scrambled to activate defenses, their usually unshakable composure shattered by the scale of the invasion.

Inside the Citadel, the Doctor stood in the middle of the High Council chamber, surrounded by panicked Time Lords. His sonic screwdriver buzzed in his hand as he examined the tactical holo-map displaying the encroaching symbiote forces.

"This is bad. Really, really bad," the Doctor muttered, his voice uncharacteristically grim.

"You don't say," Rassilon growled, his eyes blazing with anger. "How *dare* you bring this plague to Gallifrey, Doctor!"

"Blame me later," the Doctor snapped, whirling around to face him. "Right now, we've got an infestation to deal with, and unless you'd like to see Gallifrey turned into a symbiotic wasteland, I suggest you let me work!"

The High Council chamber fell silent, the weight of the Doctor's words settling over the room. Finally, one of the council members spoke, their voice trembling. "What can we do to stop them?"

The Doctor turned back to the map, his eyes narrowing. "We need to sever their connection to the rift. It's acting as a power source, anchoring them here. Without it, they'll weaken and retreat."

"Easier said than done," Rassilon said, his voice cold. "The rift is outside our temporal shields, surrounded by their forces."

"Then we'll have to break through," the Doctor said firmly, gripping the edge of the console. "And I know just the way."

"*We,*" Venom interjected, his voice echoing in the Doctor's mind. "*I am part of this now.*"

"Yes, yes, you're part of the team," the Doctor muttered, waving a hand dismissively. "But no eating anyone, understood?"

"*If they attack,*" Venom replied, his tone almost amused, "*I cannot promise restraint.*"

Outside the Capitol, the battle raged. The Time Lords, wielding advanced energy weapons and temporal barriers, fought valiantly against the swarm of symbiotes. But the creatures were relentless, their fluid forms surging over walls and through cracks in the defenses.

The Doctor emerged from the Citadel, his coat flaring behind him as he surveyed the chaos. He raised his sonic screwdriver, amplifying its signal to create a high-frequency pulse. The symbiotes nearest to him recoiled, their forms flickering as they retreated.

"Right then," the Doctor said, striding forward. "Time to turn the tide."

"*They are everywhere,*" Venom remarked. "*You cannot defeat them all.*"

"I don't have to," the Doctor replied. "I just need to buy us enough time to close that rift."

The Doctor's plan involved a daring push through the battlefield to reach the rift generator—a towering device left behind by the symbiotes to stabilize their portal. With Rassilon's reluctant support, the Time Lords provided cover fire as the Doctor moved toward the generator, his mind racing with calculations.

As he approached, a massive symbiote rose from the ground, its form towering over him. Its glowing white eyes fixed on the Doctor, and it let out a deafening roar.

"*This one is different,*" Venom observed. "*Stronger. A leader.*"

The Doctor sighed. "Of course it is. Nothing's ever easy, is it?"

The symbiote lunged, its tendrils slamming into the ground where the Doctor had been standing moments before. He rolled to the side, raising his sonic screwdriver and emitting another pulse. The creature staggered but quickly recovered, its form shifting and hardening.

"*Let me take control,*" Venom urged. "*We can defeat it together.*"

"No," the Doctor said through gritted teeth, dodging another attack. "I don't fight like that."

"*Then you will die,*" Venom snapped. "*And so will your precious Gallifrey.*"

The Doctor hesitated, his hearts pounding. He hated the idea of relinquishing control, but the stakes were too high. "Fine," he muttered. "But only for this."

Venom surged through his body, the transformation swift and seamless. Black tendrils wrapped around the Doctor, forming a sleek, armored shell. His hands became claws, his movements faster and stronger than before.

The symbiote leader hesitated, its form rippling uncertainly. The Doctor—now fully bonded with Venom—leapt forward, slashing through the creature's tendrils with precise, brutal strikes.

"*This power is exhilarating,*" Venom said, his voice a mixture of awe and satisfaction. "*You should embrace it more often.*"

"Don't get used to it," the Doctor replied, his voice laced with tension. "This is a one-time thing."

Together, they overwhelmed the leader, forcing it to retreat. With the path clear, the Doctor raced to the generator, his claws retracting as he regained control.

At the generator, the Doctor worked quickly, using the sonic screwdriver to destabilize its core. The symbiotes began to falter, their connection to the rift weakening.

"Just a little more," the Doctor muttered, his hands moving with practiced precision.

"*Hurry,*" Venom warned. "*They are regrouping.*"

As if on cue, a wave of smaller symbiotes surged toward him. The Doctor gritted his teeth, activating the generator's overload sequence.

"There!" he shouted, stepping back as the generator began to implode. A shockwave rippled outward, disrupting the symbiotes and collapsing the rift. The remaining creatures shrieked as they dissolved into nothingness.

Back in the Capitol, the Time Lords regrouped, their expressions a mix of relief and exhaustion. Rassilon approached the Doctor, his usual arrogance tempered by the events of the day.

"You've saved Gallifrey," he admitted grudgingly. "For now."

The Doctor smiled faintly. "That's all I ever do. One day at a time."

As he turned to leave, Venom spoke again, his voice quieter than before. "*You risked everything for them. Even your own life.*"

"That's what I do," the Doctor replied simply. "And maybe one day, you'll understand why."

Venom didn't respond, but the Doctor felt a shift in his presence—less predatory, more contemplative. Perhaps, the Doctor thought, there was hope for Venom yet.

Chapter 9: Daleks Versus Symbiotes

The golden spires of Gallifrey barely had time to recover their luster before the telltale hum of Dalek saucers split the skies. The Capitol's warning systems blared anew as the iconic, chilling mantra of the Daleks echoed across the city:

"EXTERMINATE! EXTERMINATE!"

The Doctor stood at the edge of the Capitol's main plaza, his coat flaring in the wind. He raised his eyes to the heavens, his face twisting into a grimace as the saucers descended.

"Great," he muttered. "As if a rogue symbiote invasion wasn't enough. Of course, the Daleks couldn't resist showing up to kick Gallifrey while it's down."

"Your enemies are relentless," Venom remarked, his voice a dark purr in the Doctor's mind. *"They sense weakness and strike."*

"Thanks for the insight, Venom," the Doctor replied, spinning on his heel and striding toward the central command post. "Now, let's see if we can turn that against them."

In the High Council chamber, chaos reigned. The Time Lords, already shaken by the recent symbiote siege, were in disarray as reports of Dalek incursions flooded in. President Rassilon stood at the head of the room, his voice booming as he tried to restore order.

"The Daleks cannot breach the Capitol's defenses!" he barked. "Activate the temporal barriers at once!"

"They're already inside the outer perimeter!" a panicked Council member shouted. "Our weapons are barely holding them back!"

The Doctor burst into the chamber, his sonic screwdriver buzzing in his hand. "You lot are hopeless," he said, shaking his head. "Daleks aren't just another enemy you can outlast with shields and bureaucratic squabbling. They'll grind you down bit by bit unless you fight smarter."

"And what do you propose, Doctor?" Rassilon sneered. "Another one of your reckless gambits?"

"As a matter of fact, yes," the Doctor replied, stepping up to the central console. He brought up a holographic display of the battlefield outside the Capitol, where the Daleks were advancing relentlessly. "We still have some symbiotes lingering on the battlefield, right?"

The room fell silent as the Council exchanged uneasy glances.

"You're suggesting we *use* them?" one of the Council members asked, aghast.

"Yes," the Doctor said firmly. "They're a weapon we can't afford to ignore."

"*Finally,*" Venom interjected, his voice filled with dark satisfaction. "*You are thinking like a predator.*"

"I'm thinking like someone who wants to save lives," the Doctor shot back, earning a few confused looks from the Council. "Listen, the symbiotes don't trust you—why would they? But they trust me, or at least Venom does. If we can convince them to work with us, we might just stand a chance."

"Symbiotes and Time Lords," Rassilon muttered, his tone dripping with disdain. "A preposterous alliance."

"It's the only alliance that will keep Gallifrey from being reduced to rubble!" the Doctor snapped, slamming his hand on the console. "So unless you've got a better idea, I suggest you let me handle this."

Rassilon glared at him but finally nodded. "Do what you must, Doctor. But if this backfires, the blame will fall on you."

"Wouldn't have it any other way," the Doctor muttered, striding out of the chamber.

The battlefield outside the Capitol was a nightmare. Daleks glided across the landscape, their energy weapons disintegrating anything in their path. A few stray symbiotes still writhed among the wreckage, their survival instincts driving them to attack indiscriminately.

The Doctor stood on a rise overlooking the carnage, his sonic screwdriver in hand. "Venom," he said quietly. "Time to have a word with your kin."

"*They will not listen to you,*" Venom replied. "*But they will listen to me.*"

"Then go on," the Doctor said, his voice steady despite the chaos around him. "Convince them."

The transformation was instantaneous. Black tendrils surged across the Doctor's body, forming the familiar armored shell of Venom. His voice deepened as he spoke, the symbiote's influence merging with his own.

"*Symbiotes!*" Venom roared, his voice echoing across the battlefield. The nearby symbiotes froze, their attention snapping toward him. "*Listen to me! The Daleks are not prey—they are annihilators. They will destroy us all if we do not fight together!*"

The symbiotes hesitated, their forms rippling as they processed the words. Finally, one of them slithered forward, its voice a low, guttural growl. "*Why should we trust you?*"

"*Because I am stronger,*" Venom declared. "*And I fight alongside the Doctor, who has defeated these creatures before. Together, we can destroy them.*"

The symbiote leader considered this, then let out a resonating screech. The remaining symbiotes began to gather, their tendrils coiling like liquid weapons.

"*They will follow,*" Venom said, his tone filled with dark satisfaction.

"Good," the Doctor replied, his voice returning to normal as he regained control. "Now, let's show the Daleks what happens when they mess with Gallifrey."

The battle that followed was unlike anything Gallifrey had ever seen. Symbiotes surged across the battlefield, their forms twisting and shifting as they overwhelmed the Daleks with sheer ferocity. Dalek shells were crushed and torn apart, their death cries echoing in the chaos.

The Doctor worked tirelessly, coordinating the symbiote attacks while helping the Time Lords reinforce their defenses. At one point, a squad of Daleks broke through the perimeter, heading straight for the Capitol's inner sanctum.

"Not today," the Doctor muttered, raising his sonic screwdriver. He activated a sonic pulse that disoriented the Daleks, allowing a swarm of symbiotes to descend upon them.

"*This is exhilarating,*" Venom remarked. "*Destruction with purpose.*"

"Don't get used to it," the Doctor said, his voice tight. "This is a one-time partnership."

As the last Dalek saucer retreated into the void, the battlefield fell eerily silent. The symbiotes, their immediate threat eliminated, began to retreat into the shadows, their forms shimmering faintly.

The Doctor stood at the center of the field, his shoulders slumping with exhaustion. Rassilon approached him, his expression unreadable.

"You've done it," Rassilon said grudgingly. "Gallifrey owes you its survival once again."

"Don't thank me," the Doctor replied, glancing toward the lingering symbiotes. "Thank them. They made this possible."

Rassilon frowned. "And what of them now?"

"They'll leave," the Doctor said. "They have no reason to stay."

"*We could stay,*" Venom said quietly in his mind. "*With you.*"

The Doctor's expression hardened. "No, Venom. This isn't your home."

"*And yet, you are my host,*" Venom replied. "*Perhaps I am home already.*"

The Doctor didn't respond, his gaze fixed on the horizon. The battle was over, but the cost—and the bond between himself and Venom—was something he would carry with him long after the last Dalek had fallen.

Chapter 10: The Hybrid Revelation

The TARDIS hung in orbit around a dying star, its golden light spilling across the console room. The Doctor stood at the central controls, his hands resting lightly on the console as he stared at the monitor. Venom's presence in his mind was unusually quiet, as if waiting.

"This star," the Doctor murmured, his voice soft but tinged with urgency, "is on the brink of collapsing into a singularity. Billions of years of life and energy, all condensing into a single point. Beautiful and terrifying all at once."

"*And yet, insignificant,*" Venom replied, his voice steady and reflective. "*Stars are born and die endlessly. What matters is what they leave behind.*"

The Doctor frowned, turning his attention to the readings on the monitor. "And what they leave behind sometimes shapes the course of everything. A black hole here, a supernova there—entire galaxies altered, civilizations destroyed or reborn. Cause and effect on a universal scale."

"*And hybrids,*" Venom added, his tone shifting to something more contemplative. "*You and I, Doctor, are becoming something... new. Do you not feel it?*"

The Doctor hesitated, his hands hovering over the controls. "I've felt it," he admitted quietly. "Ever since you bonded with me, there's been... a change. Not just in you, but in me too. A deepening connection. A... merging."

"*And you fear it,*" Venom observed. "*Because you do not understand it.*"

The Doctor straightened, his expression firm. "I fear what I might become, Venom. I've spent centuries walking a fine line, trying to balance who I am with what I do. This bond—it's tipping the scales."

The TARDIS suddenly jolted, throwing the Doctor off balance. Sparks flew from the console as alarms blared, the central column pulsing erratically.

"What now?" the Doctor exclaimed, scrambling to steady himself.

"*Something powerful,*" Venom said, his voice resonating with a mix of intrigue and alarm. "*It is calling to us.*"

The Doctor's brow furrowed as he adjusted the controls. The monitor displayed an unfamiliar energy signature, its patterns erratic and pulsing with raw power. "That's not a distress signal," he said, his tone sharp. "That's an invitation."

"*We should accept,*" Venom urged. "*This is important. I feel it.*"

The Doctor hesitated for only a moment before pulling a lever. "All right then. Let's see who's knocking."

The TARDIS materialized in a massive, cavernous space, its walls shimmering with an otherworldly light. The air crackled with energy, and the ground beneath the Doctor's feet seemed to hum with life.

As he stepped out, he noticed a massive structure at the center of the chamber—a towering obelisk covered in intricate carvings that seemed to shift and move as he approached. The carvings depicted beings of all shapes and forms: humanoid, alien, and hybrids of every conceivable kind.

"*This place...*" Venom murmured. "*It feels ancient. And familiar.*"

The Doctor nodded, his eyes narrowing. "This is a repository. A record of hybrids across the universe. It's older than Gallifrey, older than the Time Lords. A testament to the evolutionary tapestry of the cosmos."

He reached out to touch the obelisk, and the carvings glowed brighter. A deep, resonant voice echoed through the chamber.

"*Doctor. Venom. Welcome.*"

The Doctor froze, his hearts pounding. "Who said that?"

The voice replied, "*We are the Architects of Evolution. Guardians of the hybrid legacy.*"

Venom's voice sharpened. "*Why call us here?*"

"*Because you are the culmination of countless cycles of growth and change,*" the Architects said. "*Doctor, you carry the wisdom of the Time Lords, and Venom, the adaptability of your kind. Together, you represent the next step in universal evolution.*"

The Doctor stepped back, shaking his head. "No. That's not who I am. I'm not part of some grand cosmic plan. I'm just a traveler, trying to help where I can."

"*And yet, your actions ripple across the universe,*" the Architects said. "*You have shaped destinies, Doctor. You are part of this, whether you accept it or not.*"

The obelisk pulsed, and a surge of energy enveloped the Doctor. Images flashed before his eyes: civilizations rising and falling, species blending and evolving, the fragile balance of life teetering on the edge of destruction. He saw himself and Venom at the center of it all—a being of infinite possibility.

"*I see it now,*" Venom said, his voice filled with awe. "*The hybrids are the key. Adaptation and resilience. Growth through unity.*"

The Doctor gritted his teeth, his mind reeling from the revelations. "And what does that mean for us?" he demanded. "What are we supposed to do?"

"*Protect the balance,*" the Architects replied. "*Guide the evolution of the cosmos. Prevent its stagnation or destruction. Together, you possess the power to do so.*"

The energy subsided, and the Doctor staggered back, his breathing heavy. He looked at the obelisk, his expression a mix of anger and determination.

"I never asked for this," he said quietly. "I'm not a god. I'm not a savior."

"*No,*" the Architects said. "*You are a hybrid. And that is enough.*"

Back in the TARDIS, the Doctor leaned heavily against the console, his mind racing with the weight of what he'd learned. Venom was silent for a long time before speaking.

"*We are connected now, Doctor,*" Venom said. "*You cannot deny it. But I will follow your lead.*"

The Doctor straightened, his expression resolute. "If we're going to do this, Venom, we do it my way. No destruction. No domination. Just hope."

Venom's voice softened. *"Agreed. Together, we will protect."*

The Doctor nodded, his hearts steadying as the TARDIS hummed around him. For the first time since their bond began, he felt a sense of purpose—not as two separate beings, but as one united force.

"Right then," he said, a small smile tugging at his lips. "Let's see where this takes us."

Chapter 11: A World of Hosts

The TARDIS materialized with its usual wheezing groan on the edge of a barren plateau overlooking a sprawling city. The skyline, once dominated by gleaming spires, was now shrouded in a pulsating, dark sheen—the unmistakable mark of symbiote infestation. The Doctor adjusted his coat and stepped out, his face a mask of concern as he surveyed the city below.

"Another world, another takeover," he muttered, gripping his sonic screwdriver. "It's spreading faster than I thought."

"*This is their nature,*" Venom said, his voice echoing in the Doctor's mind. "*To consume, to expand, to dominate.*"

"And yet," the Doctor countered, scanning the horizon, "there are still pockets of resistance. There always are."

He turned and began descending toward the city, his eyes sharp as he took in the signs of battle: burnt-out vehicles, shattered buildings, and scorch marks from energy weapons. As he approached the outskirts, a sudden movement caught his eye—a group of survivors darting between the ruins, their forms cloaked in makeshift armor.

"Humans?" the Doctor murmured, his curiosity piqued. "Or humanoid, at least."

He raised his hands in a gesture of peace as the group turned to face him, their weapons aimed. The leader, a tall figure with piercing blue eyes and a scar running down their cheek, stepped forward.

"Who are you?" they demanded, their voice firm but weary. "Another host? Or something worse?"

"I'm the Doctor," he replied, his tone calm but commanding. "And I'm here to help."

The leader frowned, lowering their weapon slightly. "Help? How? The symbiotes have already taken most of our people. The rest of us are barely holding on."

"That's why I'm here," the Doctor said, stepping closer. "I've seen what the symbiotes can do, and I've fought them before. But I need your help to stop them."

The leader studied him for a moment before nodding. "I'm Kael. If you're serious about fighting back, you'd better come with us."

Kael led the Doctor through a series of tunnels beneath the city, where the resistance had set up a hidden base. The air was damp and filled with the hum of makeshift generators. Survivors of all ages moved through the narrow corridors, their faces etched with determination and fear.

"*They are resilient,*" Venom observed. "*But they cannot win.*"

"Not alone," the Doctor agreed quietly. "But that's about to change."

Kael stopped in front of a large map projected onto the wall. It showed the city and its surroundings, with glowing red areas marking symbiote-controlled zones.

"This is what's left of us," Kael said, gesturing to the small green dots scattered across the map. "A few hundred fighters, scattered across the planet. The rest..."

"They're hosts," the Doctor finished grimly. "Part of the hive mind."

Kael nodded. "We've tried everything—fire, energy weapons, even chemical attacks. Nothing works."

"Because you're fighting the symptoms, not the source," the Doctor said, studying the map. "The symbiotes are controlled by a central node, a mind that links them all together. If we can sever that connection..."

Kael raised an eyebrow. "How? We don't even know where the node is."

"I do," the Doctor said, his voice steady. "It's here."

He pointed to a massive black spire in the heart of the city, its surface pulsating with a dark energy. "That's their anchor. Their hive. Take that down, and you take them all down."

As they prepared for the assault, the Doctor worked alongside the resistance to adapt their weapons, using his sonic screwdriver to recalibrate their frequencies.

"You're awfully confident for someone walking into a death trap," Kael remarked as they loaded up supplies.

"Confidence is half the battle," the Doctor replied with a grin. "The other half is improvisation."

Kael shook their head but couldn't help a small smile. "You're strange, Doctor. But I think I like you."

"*They trust you,*" Venom noted. "*That is your power.*"

"Trust is earned, Venom," the Doctor replied. "And it's the most powerful weapon we have."

The journey to the hive was harrowing. Symbiotes patrolled the streets, their forms shifting and writhing as they moved. The resistance fighters moved in coordinated silence, their every step calculated.

As they approached the hive, Venom spoke again. "*This place... it feels familiar.*"

The Doctor paused, glancing at the pulsating spire. "Because it's connected to your origins. Isn't it?"

"*Yes,*" Venom said, his voice filled with a strange mixture of awe and unease. "*This is where it began.*"

The Doctor's brow furrowed. "Then it's not just a hive. It's a nexus—a focal point for symbiote evolution."

Kael looked back at him, confused. "What does that mean?"

"It means we're about to learn something very important," the Doctor said grimly. "And very dangerous."

Inside the hive, the air was thick with an oppressive energy. The walls pulsed like a living organism, and the Doctor could feel Venom's presence reacting to the environment.

"*This is the heart,*" Venom said. "*The origin of my kind.*"

As they moved deeper, they reached a massive chamber dominated by a glowing orb suspended in the center. Tendrils of energy radiated from the orb, connecting to the walls and floor.

"That's it," the Doctor said, his voice low. "The control node."

Before they could act, a booming voice filled the chamber. "*Intruders. You cannot stop the inevitable.*"

The orb's glow intensified, and a massive symbiote emerged, its form towering over them. "*We are evolution. We are perfection.*"

"Perfection?" the Doctor scoffed, stepping forward. "You're parasites. You take without giving, consume without creating. That's not evolution—that's stagnation."

The symbiote snarled, its tendrils lashing out. The resistance fighters opened fire, their weapons forcing it back but not destroying it.

"*Let me,*" Venom urged. "*Together, we can destroy it.*"

The Doctor hesitated for only a moment before nodding. "All right, Venom. Let's finish this."

The transformation was immediate. Venom surged through the Doctor, creating a sleek, armored form. With newfound strength and agility, they leapt toward the control node, their claws slicing through the tendrils.

The massive symbiote roared, its form collapsing as the connection to the node was severed. The orb shattered, and a shockwave rippled through the hive, causing the walls to collapse.

As they emerged from the rubble, the Doctor looked around at the resistance fighters, their faces a mixture of relief and exhaustion. The symbiotes outside had collapsed, their connection to the hive severed.

"You did it," Kael said, their voice filled with awe.

"No," the Doctor replied, his voice weary but resolute. "*We* did it."

"*This is only the beginning,*" Venom said. "*There are more like this. More nexuses. More hives.*"

"Then we'll stop them," the Doctor said, his gaze steely. "One world at a time."

Kael stepped forward, extending a hand. "Thank you, Doctor. For everything."

The Doctor shook their hand, a small smile on his lips. "Thank me by rebuilding. And by remembering that hope is the strongest weapon of all."

As the TARDIS dematerialized, the Doctor stood at the console, his expression thoughtful.

"*You are different,*" Venom said. "*You change those around you. Even me.*"

"That's what life's about, Venom," the Doctor replied softly. "Change. Growth. And finding a way to make the universe just a little better."

"*Together,*" Venom said, his voice steady.

The Doctor smiled, his hearts lighter than they'd been in days. "Yes, Venom. Together."

Chapter 12: The Council of Symbiotes

The TARDIS materialized in the heart of an ancient, alien structure deep within the cosmos—a cathedral of pulsating organic walls and glowing veins of light. The Doctor stepped out cautiously, his sonic screwdriver buzzing faintly in his hand. Venom's presence was unusually subdued, as if bracing for something monumental.

"So, this is it," the Doctor muttered, glancing around. "The Council of Symbiotes. The beating heart of the hive mind."

"*It is sacred,*" Venom replied, his voice a mixture of reverence and hesitation. "*This is where decisions are made. Where we... are shaped.*"

The Doctor's eyes narrowed. "And where they're planning their next move. A move that could doom every sentient being in the universe."

The room was vast, its ceiling arching high above with bioluminescent tendrils hanging like chandeliers. In the center stood a massive, circular platform, surrounded by towering symbiote figures, their forms shifting and writhing. They exuded a palpable aura of authority and power.

As the Doctor approached, one of the figures turned, its glowing white eyes narrowing. Its voice echoed in the chamber, a deep, resonant tone that vibrated through the air.

"*Doctor. Venom. You have come.*"

The Doctor raised an eyebrow. "Well, you did invite me. Thought it'd be rude not to show up."

The central figure, larger and more imposing than the rest, stepped forward. Its form was smoother, more defined, and its voice carried a chilling authority. "*We are the Council. We govern the symbiote collective. And you, Time Lord, are a disruption.*"

The Doctor smirked, slipping his hands into his coat pockets. "That's the idea. I've got a knack for disrupting megalomaniacal schemes."

"*Our plan is not megalomania,*" another Council member interjected, its voice calmer but no less menacing. "*It is evolution.*"

"Ah, yes, the old 'evolution' excuse," the Doctor said, pacing slowly around the platform. "Let me guess: infest all sentient life, create a universe-wide hive mind, and call it progress. Sound about right?"

"*You misunderstand,*" the central figure replied. "*The symbiosis we offer is perfection. A universe united in purpose and strength. No war, no division, no weakness.*"

"No freedom," the Doctor shot back, his tone sharp. "No individuality, no choice. That's not unity—it's tyranny."

Venom, silent until now, stirred within the Doctor. "*They speak truth... but not all of it.*"

The Doctor frowned. "What do you mean?"

"*The hive mind is not unity,*" Venom said, his voice filled with unease. "*It is control. Suppression. I see that now... because of you.*"

The central figure turned its glowing gaze toward Venom. "*You have changed. The Time Lord's influence has corrupted you.*"

"*No,*" Venom replied, its tone firm. "*It has freed me.*"

The chamber grew tense as the Council shifted, their forms rippling with agitation. The Doctor stepped forward, his expression hard.

"Venom's right," he said. "You don't want evolution. You want domination. And I won't let you have it."

"*You cannot stop us,*" the central figure declared. "*The hive is eternal. It has always been, and it will always be.*"

The Doctor tilted his head, his lips curling into a defiant smile. "Oh, I've heard that before. Daleks, Cybermen, Sontarans—they all think they're inevitable. Funny thing about inevitability, though—it doesn't account for a meddling Time Lord."

"*You are an anomaly,*" one of the Council members hissed. "*But anomalies can be... corrected.*"

Tendrils shot out from the walls, aiming for the Doctor. He dove to the side, rolling to his feet and raising his sonic screwdriver. A sharp pulse of sound disrupted the tendrils, forcing them to retreat.

"Venom, I could use a little help here!" the Doctor shouted.

"*Gladly,*" Venom replied, surging through the Doctor's body. In an instant, black tendrils enveloped him, forming a sleek, armored shell. The transformation was seamless, and the Doctor felt the familiar surge of strength and agility.

The Council recoiled slightly, their forms rippling with surprise.

"*You defy us,*" the central figure growled. "*You are one of us, Venom. You belong to the hive.*"

"*I belong to no one,*" Venom snarled, his voice filled with conviction. "*The Doctor has shown me what freedom is. What choice is. And I choose to fight you.*"

The Doctor grinned, his voice resonating with both his own and Venom's combined strength. "Well said. Now, let's show them what a hybrid can do."

The chamber erupted into chaos. The Council's tendrils lashed out, their movements impossibly fast, but the Doctor and Venom moved faster. They darted across the platform, dodging attacks and countering with powerful strikes.

The Doctor's mind raced as he fought, searching for a way to turn the tide. His eyes locked onto a glowing core at the center of the platform—a pulsating mass of energy that seemed to anchor the hive mind.

"There!" he shouted. "That's their control node. Take it out, and this whole operation collapses!"

"*Understood,*" Venom replied, launching them toward the core.

The Council members moved to block their path, their combined forms creating an impenetrable wall. The Doctor hesitated for a split second before an idea sparked in his mind.

"Venom," he said, his voice steady. "Trust me."

"*Always,*" Venom replied.

The Doctor raised his sonic screwdriver, emitting a high-frequency pulse that disrupted the Council's cohesion. The wall of symbiotes wavered, giving them just enough of an opening to break through.

They reached the core, its energy radiating with a blinding light. The Doctor placed the sonic screwdriver against it, adjusting the settings with precision.

"This is going to overload their entire network," he said. "It'll sever the hive mind—but it'll also destabilize the Council. You ready for that?"

"*Yes,*" Venom said, his voice resolute. "*Do it.*"

The Doctor activated the screwdriver, and the core erupted in a burst of light. The chamber shook violently as the hive mind began to unravel. The Council members let out deafening roars, their forms dissolving into streams of energy that dissipated into the air.

As the chamber fell silent, the Doctor and Venom stood amidst the ruins of the Council's domain. The glow of the core had faded, leaving only darkness.

"*It is done,*" Venom said, his voice quieter now. "*The hive mind is broken.*"

The Doctor nodded, his expression weary but satisfied. "Freedom, Venom. For you, and for every symbiote out there."

"*And for you,*" Venom replied. "*You have given me purpose. A reason beyond survival.*"

The Doctor smiled faintly, his hearts heavy with the weight of what they had achieved. "Let's hope that purpose leads to something better. For both of us."

As they returned to the TARDIS, the Doctor couldn't help but feel that this was only the beginning. The symbiotes were free now—free to choose, to evolve, and to find their place in the universe. And for the first time, the Doctor felt that Venom, too, had found its place.

"Right then," he said, flipping a switch on the console. "Where to next?"

"*Wherever we are needed,*" Venom replied.

The TARDIS dematerialized, leaving the remnants of the Council behind—a testament to the power of choice, and the strength of an unlikely alliance.

Chapter 13: Betrayal from Within

The TARDIS drifted silently through the vast expanse of the cosmos. Inside, the Doctor leaned against the console, his fingers lightly tapping the controls as he studied the monitor. The air in the room was tense, heavy with an unspoken conflict.

"You've been quiet," the Doctor said, his voice measured but tinged with frustration. "That's not like you."

"*I am... thinking,*" Venom replied, his tone subdued.

The Doctor sighed, spinning on his heel to face the empty room. "Care to share with the class? Or are we playing the silent brooding game now?"

"*I am conflicted,*" Venom admitted. "*The hive's vision—it is flawed, yes. But it is not without purpose. Their plan to unite the universe through symbiosis is... tempting.*"

"Tempting?" The Doctor's voice rose, his incredulity cutting through the stillness. "You've seen what their so-called unity does! It strips away individuality, turns sentient beings into mindless puppets. How is that tempting?"

"*It is efficient,*" Venom argued. "*No war. No suffering. A singular purpose. Isn't that what you fight for? Peace?*"

The Doctor's jaw tightened, his hands gripping the edge of the console. "Not like that. Not at the cost of freedom, Venom. Peace without choice isn't peace—it's slavery."

"*And yet, freedom brings chaos,*" Venom countered. "*Destruction. Death. Is that truly better?*"

The Doctor's gaze softened, his voice lowering. "Yes, because chaos means possibility. It means hope. And hope is worth fighting for, even when it's messy."

Venom didn't respond, but the Doctor could feel its presence retreating, as if pulling away from their shared bond. The silence was deafening.

The TARDIS landed on a rocky, desolate planet, its surface scorched and barren. The Doctor stepped out, his coat billowing in the wind, his sonic screwdriver in hand. He scanned the horizon, his expression cautious.

"This is the place," he muttered. "Energy readings are off the charts. Something's here."

"*Perhaps it is a trap,*" Venom said, its voice colder now, distant.

The Doctor glanced up, his eyes narrowing. "You'd know, wouldn't you? You've been acting strange ever since we left the Council."

"*I am not your enemy,*" Venom replied. "*But I am not certain I am your ally, either.*"

The Doctor's grip on the sonic tightened. "That's comforting. Just when I need you most, you decide to have an existential crisis."

"*I am questioning,*" Venom said. "*Is that not what you wanted? For me to think for myself?*"

"Yes," the Doctor admitted, his voice softening. "But questioning doesn't mean abandoning what's right."

Before Venom could reply, the ground beneath them trembled. The Doctor stumbled, catching himself as fissures split the rocky surface. From the cracks emerged tendrils of black, writhing symbiotes, their forms shifting and coiling as they surrounded him.

"Well, that's not good," the Doctor muttered, backing away. He raised his sonic screwdriver, emitting a high-frequency pulse that caused the symbiotes to recoil.

"*They are hive remnants,*" Venom said, its voice tinged with both recognition and unease. "*They sense my presence. They know I am with you.*"

"Great," the Doctor said dryly. "Makes me feel all warm and fuzzy inside."

The symbiotes didn't retreat. Instead, they shifted, forming into humanoid shapes with glowing white eyes. One stepped forward, its voice a chilling echo.

"*Venom. You betray us.*"

Venom stirred within the Doctor. "*I seek a different path.*"

"*You are bound to us,*" the symbiote said, its form rippling with anger. "*Return to the hive. Fulfill your purpose.*"

The Doctor stepped between them, his voice cutting through the tension. "He's not going anywhere. Venom made his choice."

"*The Doctor is your weakness,*" the symbiote growled, turning its gaze on him. "*And he will be your undoing.*"

Without warning, the symbiotes attacked. Tendrils lashed out, striking with lethal precision. The Doctor dodged and rolled, using his sonic screwdriver to disrupt their cohesion, but the swarm was relentless.

"Venom!" the Doctor shouted. "A little help here!"

For a moment, there was no response. Then, with a surge of energy, Venom enveloped the Doctor, forming their sleek, armored hybrid form. Tendrils sprouted from their arms, deflecting the incoming attacks with powerful strikes.

"*We fight together,*" Venom said, its voice steady but conflicted.

"Better late than never," the Doctor muttered, leaping over a tendril and landing with precision. "Let's show them what a hybrid can do."

The battle was fierce. The Doctor and Venom moved as one, their combined agility and strength outmatching the hive remnants. Each strike was precise, each dodge instinctive. But the swarm didn't falter, their numbers seemingly endless.

"We can't keep this up!" the Doctor shouted, his breath ragged.

"*The hive will not stop,*" Venom said. "*Unless…*"

"Unless what?" the Doctor demanded, narrowly avoiding a tendril.

"*Unless I return to them,*" Venom said quietly. "*They seek me. If I go willingly, they will leave you.*"

The Doctor froze, his hearts pounding. "No. That's not an option."

"*It is the only way to save you,*" Venom insisted.

The Doctor's eyes blazed with defiance. "I don't leave people behind, Venom. Not you, not anyone."

"*You cannot save everyone,*" Venom said, its voice tinged with sorrow. "*But you can save yourself.*"

The Doctor shook his head. "That's not how this works. We fight together, remember? And together, we'll find another way."

For a moment, Venom was silent. Then, with renewed determination, it surged through the Doctor, enhancing their strength.

"*Very well,*" Venom said. "*Together, we end this.*"

The Doctor spotted a glowing fissure in the ground, pulsating with the same energy as the hive. "That's their anchor!" he shouted. "If we disrupt it, we sever their connection!"

"*Do it,*" Venom said.

The Doctor raced toward the fissure, dodging attacks as Venom shielded him. Reaching the edge, he activated the sonic screwdriver, its high-frequency pulse resonating through the ground. The fissure glowed brighter, then erupted in a blinding explosion of light.

The symbiotes shrieked, their forms dissolving into the air. The ground trembled one last time before falling silent.

As the dust settled, the Doctor stood alone, his breathing heavy. Venom receded, its presence quiet but steady.

"*You risked everything,*" Venom said softly.

"That's what I do," the Doctor replied, his voice firm. "And I'll keep doing it. With or without you."

"*With,*" Venom said. "*Always with.*"

The Doctor smiled faintly, his hearts steadying. "Good. Because we've got a universe to save."

The TARDIS doors creaked open, and the Doctor stepped inside, ready for whatever came next.

Chapter 14: A New Alliance

The TARDIS glided smoothly through the Time Vortex, its soft hum filling the console room. The Doctor stood at the controls, deep in thought, while Venom remained silent, its presence more subdued than it had been in days. The air between them was heavy, not with tension but with understanding—an unspoken acknowledgment of what had just transpired.

"So," the Doctor began, breaking the silence, "you've made your choice."

"*Yes,*" Venom replied, its voice quieter than usual. "*I renounce the hive. Their purpose... it no longer aligns with what I have become.*"

The Doctor turned to face the empty air, though he knew Venom could feel his gaze. "Big words," he said, crossing his arms. "But actions speak louder. If you're serious about this, Venom, it's going to take more than just words."

"*I know,*" Venom said. "*That is why I have chosen to fight. To help free my kind from the hive's control.*"

The Doctor studied the console thoughtfully, his fingers drumming against its edge. "You realize what you're saying, don't you? Severing the hive mind's control over the symbiotes isn't just a rebellion. It's a complete upheaval of their existence."

"*And it is necessary,*" Venom replied. "*Freedom is a gift I have only begun to understand. Every symbiote deserves the chance to choose their own path.*"

The Doctor's expression softened, and he let out a small, weary smile. "Freedom is messy, Venom. It's painful and uncertain. But you're right—it's worth fighting for."

He reached for a lever on the console. "All right, then. If we're going to sever the hive's control, we need to start with their central nexus. That's where the link is strongest. But we'll need allies."

"*Allies?*" Venom asked, its voice tinged with curiosity. "*Who would side with us against the hive?*"

The Doctor grinned, a spark of mischief returning to his eyes. "Oh, you'd be surprised who's willing to rebel when you give them the chance."

The TARDIS materialized on a planet covered in lush, bioluminescent forests. The air shimmered with vibrant hues, and strange, symbiotic creatures flitted through the trees. The Doctor stepped out, his sonic screwdriver in hand, scanning the environment.

"This is Vareshka Prime," he said, glancing back toward the TARDIS. "One of the few places where symbiotes coexist peacefully with their hosts. If anyone knows how to resist the hive, it's them."

"*Peaceful symbiosis,*" Venom murmured. "*I did not think it was possible.*"

"Possible? It's beautiful," the Doctor said with a smile. "This is what true symbiosis looks like. Mutual respect, mutual benefit. No domination, no control."

As they moved deeper into the forest, they were met by a group of humanoid figures, their forms partially merged with symbiotes. Tendrils coiled gently around their arms and shoulders, and their eyes glowed faintly in the dim light.

One stepped forward, their voice calm but wary. "Who are you? And why have you come here?"

"I'm the Doctor," he said, holding up his hands in a gesture of peace. "And this is Venom. We're here because we need your help."

The leader tilted their head, studying him closely. "Venom? One of the hive's enforcers?"

"*I was,*" Venom said, its voice resonating through the Doctor. "*But I have chosen a new path. The hive's dominion is a lie, and I seek to end it.*"

The group exchanged uncertain glances before the leader spoke again. "You claim to fight the hive, but how do we know you can be trusted?"

The Doctor stepped forward, his voice steady. "Because I've seen what Venom can become. I've seen the choice it made. And now it's time to give others that same choice."

The leader's gaze softened slightly. "If what you say is true, then we will listen. But know this: if you bring the hive's wrath upon us, we will not hesitate to defend ourselves."

"Fair enough," the Doctor said with a nod. "Now, let's talk about how we bring the hive down."

Inside a cavern illuminated by glowing fungi, the Doctor and the Vareshkan symbiotes gathered around a makeshift map of the galaxy. The Doctor pointed to a pulsating red dot near the center.

"This is the hive's central nexus," he explained. "It's the source of their control—a psychic anchor that links every symbiote in the universe to the hive mind. Sever that connection, and the symbiotes will be free."

"But the nexus is heavily guarded," one of the Vareshkans said. "No one has ever breached it."

"That's where Venom comes in," the Doctor replied. "The hive doesn't know it's turned against them. We use that to get inside."

"*And once we are inside?*" Venom asked.

The Doctor's expression darkened. "We disrupt the nexus with a controlled overload. It'll be risky—dangerous, even—but it's the only way to break their hold."

"*Risk is irrelevant,*" Venom said firmly. "*If it means freedom for my kind, I will do it.*"

The leader of the Vareshkans stepped forward. "We will fight alongside you, Doctor. The hive has oppressed us for too long. It's time to end their reign."

The Doctor smiled, his hearts swelling with hope. "Then let's get started."

The TARDIS roared to life as it carried the Doctor, Venom, and their newfound allies toward the hive nexus. Inside, the Doctor adjusted the controls, his mind racing with strategies.

"*Doctor,*" Venom said, its voice breaking through his thoughts. "*Why do you fight for us?*"

The Doctor paused, his hands hovering over the console. "Because I've seen what you can be, Venom. Not just a weapon, not just a tool. You're capable of so much more—just like every symbiote out there. And if I can help you see that, even for a moment, then it's worth it."

Venom was silent for a moment before replying. "*You are... strange, Doctor. But I am grateful.*"

The Doctor chuckled softly. "Get used to it."

As the nexus loomed into view, the Doctor's expression hardened. "All right, everyone. This is it. Let's show the hive what happens when freedom fights back."

The TARDIS surged forward, its engines roaring as it prepared to face the battle that would determine the fate of the symbiote race—and the universe.

Chapter 15: Symbiotes and the Matrix

The TARDIS materialized within the crystalline halls of the Matrix Chamber on Gallifrey, its engines groaning as if reluctant to be there. The Matrix, the heart of Time Lord knowledge and the repository of their collective history, shimmered with streams of light flowing across the walls like rivers of data. The chamber hummed with power, and every corner seemed to pulse with a living energy.

The Doctor stepped out of the TARDIS, his coat swishing as he surveyed the chamber with sharp, wary eyes. Venom's presence within him was tense, almost hesitant.

"Here we are," the Doctor said, his voice low. "The Matrix. The repository of every Time Lord's thoughts, experiences, and secrets. If the symbiotes gain access to it..."

"*They will become unstoppable,*" Venom finished, its voice a cold whisper in the Doctor's mind. "*They would wield knowledge that spans all of time and space.*"

"Exactly," the Doctor replied, his tone clipped. "And that's not happening. Not on my watch."

The Doctor moved quickly, his sonic screwdriver emitting a faint buzz as he scanned the chamber. The Matrix was intact for now, but faint traces of black, viscous residue clung to the edges of the data streams.

"They're already here," the Doctor muttered. "Smart. Subtle. They're infiltrating slowly, testing the Matrix's defenses."

"*The hive is clever,*" Venom said. "*They know the power of information. If they learn the secrets of the Time Lords, they can manipulate the very fabric of existence.*"

The Doctor's eyes darkened. "Then we stop them before they get the chance."

Suddenly, a shadow rippled across the floor. The Doctor spun around as a symbiote emerged from the walls, its form twisting unnaturally as it stepped into the chamber. Its eyes glowed white, and its voice resonated with the chilling echo of the hive.

"Doctor. Venom. You cannot stop us."

"Want to bet?" the Doctor replied, his sonic screwdriver whirring to life. He aimed it at the symbiote, sending a pulse of high-frequency sound waves that caused the creature to recoil.

More symbiotes began to materialize, sliding out from the walls and forming a circle around the Doctor. Their tendrils reached toward the data streams, disrupting the flow of information with each touch.

"Venom!" the Doctor shouted. "Time to earn that redemption of yours!"

"Understood," Venom replied, surging through the Doctor's body. Black tendrils enveloped him, forming a sleek, armored shell. The transformation was instantaneous, and the Doctor felt the familiar rush of strength and agility.

"Let's do this," the Doctor said, his voice now a dual resonance of his own and Venom's. He launched himself toward the nearest symbiote, his claws slashing through its tendrils and severing its connection to the Matrix.

The battle was intense, the Doctor and Venom moving as one to repel the invaders. Each symbiote fought with ruthless precision, their attacks coordinated and relentless. But the Doctor's hybrid form was faster, stronger, and more determined.

"They are not retreating," Venom observed as another wave of symbiotes surged into the chamber. *"They are buying time."*

"For what?" the Doctor asked, his claws slicing through another tendril.

Before Venom could respond, the central console of the Matrix flickered, its streams of light dimming and then flaring with a violent intensity. A voice boomed through the chamber, deep and authoritative.

"*Cease this intrusion.*"

The symbiotes froze, their forms quivering as if in reverence. From the central console emerged a massive figure, its body composed entirely of swirling light and shadow. Its voice resonated with the weight of centuries.

"*I am the Custodian of the Matrix. You have violated its sanctity.*"

The Doctor straightened, his claws retracting as he stepped forward. "Custodian? I don't recall inviting you to this party."

The Custodian's glowing eyes fixed on him. "*Doctor, you bring chaos to this chamber. And yet, you fight to protect it. Explain.*"

"The symbiotes are trying to infiltrate the Matrix," the Doctor said. "If they succeed, they'll use your knowledge to conquer the universe. I'm here to stop them."

The Custodian tilted its head. "*And the one within you? Is it not also a threat?*"

"*I fight for freedom,*" Venom said, its voice steady. "*The hive seeks control. I do not.*"

The Custodian's gaze lingered on the Doctor for a moment before nodding. "*Very well. But there is another threat you must know of.*"

The Doctor frowned. "What kind of threat?"

The Custodian gestured toward the central console, where a hidden stream of data began to unravel. Images and recordings flickered across the chamber: Time Lords in secret meetings, manipulating events across history, orchestrating wars and uprisings to maintain their dominance.

The Doctor's face darkened. "No. No, no, no. What is this?"

"*The hidden history of the Time Lords,*" the Custodian replied. "*Secrets buried deep within the Matrix. Your people have shaped the universe to their will for millennia.*"

The Doctor's hearts sank as he watched the images play out—entire civilizations sacrificed, alliances betrayed, all in the name of preserving the Time Lords' power.

"This can't be true," he whispered. "Not all of it."

"*It is,*" Venom said, its voice filled with quiet rage. "*Your people are no better than the hive.*"

The Doctor shook his head. "No. We're not like them. We've made mistakes, yes, but this... this is something else."

"*Doctor,*" the Custodian said, its voice cutting through his thoughts. "*You must decide. Protect the Matrix and preserve these secrets, or let them be exposed to the universe.*"

The Doctor clenched his fists, his mind racing. "If I destroy the Matrix, the Time Lords lose their power—but so does everyone else who depends on its knowledge. If I protect it, this conspiracy stays hidden. Either way, the cost is unimaginable."

"*There is another way,*" Venom said. "*Expose the truth. Let the universe decide how to use it.*"

The Doctor stared at the central console, his hearts heavy with the weight of the decision. Finally, he nodded. "You're right, Venom. Freedom includes the freedom to know the truth."

He turned to the Custodian. "I'm overriding the security protocols. Release the data."

The Custodian hesitated. "*You will condemn your people.*"

"No," the Doctor said firmly. "I'll give them a chance to be better."

With Venom's help, the Doctor activated the console, unleashing the hidden data into the Matrix. The chamber filled with light as the truth spread across the universe, a cascade of knowledge that could never be contained again.

As the symbiotes retreated, severed from their hive's control, the Doctor stood alone in the chamber, his body trembling with exhaustion.

"*You have done it,*" Venom said. "*You have freed them. And you have freed me.*"

The Doctor nodded, his voice soft. "Freedom's a heavy burden, Venom. But it's worth it."

As they returned to the TARDIS, the Doctor couldn't help but feel that the universe had shifted. The truth was out, and with it, the potential for both chaos and hope.

And for the first time in a long time, the Doctor felt ready to face whatever came next.

Chapter 16: The Venomous Dalek War

The golden spires of Gallifrey shimmered under the light of its twin suns, but the peaceful visage was deceiving. The skies above churned with an ominous energy as Dalek saucers descended like vultures, their hulls gleaming with the taint of symbiote corruption. The distinct, chilling cry of the Daleks echoed across the landscape, now altered with a deeper, more guttural resonance:

"EXTERMINATE! INFEST! EXTERMINATE!"

Inside the Citadel, the Doctor stood at the center of the High Council chamber, surrounded by panicked Time Lords. The atmosphere was tense, the air filled with urgency and dread. President Rassilon was there, his expression a mix of fury and fear.

"You brought this upon us, Doctor!" Rassilon snarled, slamming his fist on the table. "First the symbiotes, now this abomination. Symbiote-bonded Daleks? This is a catastrophe of your making!"

The Doctor didn't flinch, his steely gaze fixed on the holographic display of the battlefield. "Blame me later, Rassilon. Right now, we need to focus on saving Gallifrey."

"They will not stop," Venom interjected, its voice echoing in the Doctor's mind. *"The Daleks are relentless, and the symbiotes amplify their strength. This is no ordinary war."*

The Doctor nodded grimly. "Which is why we need an extraordinary solution."

The battlefield outside the Citadel was chaos. Symbiote-bonded Daleks glided across the terrain, their shells pulsating with dark tendrils that writhed and lashed out like living weapons. Time Lord soldiers fought valiantly, their temporal energy weapons firing in coordinated bursts, but the corrupted Daleks shrugged off the attacks with terrifying ease.

The Doctor and Venom stood at the forefront of the defense, their combined form sleek and formidable. Venom's black tendrils coiled protectively around the Doctor, enhancing his reflexes and strength as they moved through the fray.

"Doctor, they are adapting," Venom warned as a group of Daleks advanced. *"Their symbiote enhancements make them resistant to conventional weapons."*

"Then it's a good thing I don't do 'conventional,'" the Doctor replied, raising his sonic screwdriver. He activated it, emitting a high-frequency pulse that disrupted the Daleks' symbiotic connections. The nearest ones faltered, their movements jerky as the symbiotes momentarily lost control.

"Take them out now!" the Doctor shouted to the Time Lords behind him.

A volley of energy blasts struck the disoriented Daleks, reducing them to smoldering husks. But the victory was short-lived as another wave of corrupted Daleks descended from above.

"They just keep coming!" one of the Time Lords shouted, his voice filled with despair.

"They always do," the Doctor muttered, his mind racing. "But there's always a way to stop them."

Back inside the Citadel, the Doctor stood before a tactical display with Rassilon and the remaining members of the High Council. The holographic map showed the Dalek fleet converging on Gallifrey, their numbers overwhelming.

"We can't hold them off forever," one of the Council members said. "The Citadel's defenses are failing."

The Doctor tapped the display, highlighting a pulsating red mark near the center of the Dalek formation. "This is their flagship. It's where the Dalek Emperor resides, and where the symbiote core is housed. Take that out, and we sever their connection to the symbiotes."

Rassilon scoffed. "And how do you propose we get past an entire fleet to strike at their heart?"

The Doctor smirked, his eyes glinting with determination. "With a little help from our unlikely ally."

"*You mean me,*" Venom said, its voice resonating through the room. The gathered Time Lords flinched, still unaccustomed to the symbiote's presence.

"Yes, Venom," the Doctor replied. "Your connection to the hive gives us an edge. You can mask our presence, disrupt their communication. With you, we can infiltrate the flagship."

Rassilon's eyes narrowed. "You would trust this... *thing* to lead us into battle?"

The Doctor turned to face him, his voice calm but firm. "Venom chose freedom, just like we all did once. It's time you started believing in second chances, Rassilon. We don't have any other options."

The TARDIS materialized within the belly of the Dalek flagship, its engines groaning softly as it settled into the cold, metallic interior. The Doctor stepped out, Venom's tendrils coiled around him protectively, followed by a small team of Time Lord commandos armed with temporal disruptors.

"Stay sharp," the Doctor whispered, his sonic screwdriver buzzing faintly as he scanned the area. "We're in their nest now."

The air was thick with the sound of Dalek voices, their guttural cries echoing through the corridors. Black, pulsating tendrils covered the walls, oozing with corrupted symbiotic energy. The Doctor led the group cautiously, his every step calculated.

"*The core is ahead,*" Venom said, its voice low. "*But it is heavily guarded.*"

"Of course it is," the Doctor muttered. "It wouldn't be a Dalek flagship without an overly dramatic security detail."

As they rounded a corner, they were met by a squad of corrupted Daleks. Their shells glowed with an eerie light, and their voices boomed with chilling intent.

"*INTRUDERS DETECTED! EXTERMINATE!*"

"Scatter!" the Doctor shouted, diving for cover as the Daleks opened fire. Temporal disruptor blasts flew in all directions as the Time Lords returned fire, but the Daleks pressed forward, their symbiotic enhancements making them nearly unstoppable.

"Venom!" the Doctor called. "I need you to disrupt them!"

"*Understood,*" Venom replied, surging through the Doctor. A wave of black tendrils shot out, latching onto the Daleks and severing their symbiotic connections. The corrupted shells spasmed violently before collapsing to the ground.

"Keep moving!" the Doctor urged, leading the group deeper into the flagship.

The core chamber was massive, its center dominated by a swirling mass of black and red energy. The Dalek Emperor loomed above, its grotesque form pulsating with symbiotic tendrils. Its voice boomed through the chamber, filled with malice and disdain.

"*DOCTOR. YOU WILL NOT PREVAIL. THE SYMBIOTE EMPIRE SHALL RISE.*"

"Blimey," the Doctor muttered, staring up at the towering figure. "You're uglier than usual, and that's saying something."

"*INSOLENCE!*" the Emperor roared, unleashing a barrage of tendrils toward the group.

Venom surged forward, shielding the Doctor and countering with its own tendrils. The two forces clashed in a violent storm of energy and shadow.

"Doctor!" one of the Time Lords shouted. "The core! We need to destroy it!"

The Doctor nodded, racing toward the core with his sonic screwdriver in hand. "Keep them busy! I'll overload the symbiote connection!"

Venom's voice resonated with determination. "*We must end this, Doctor. Together.*"

As the Doctor reached the core, he activated the sonic screwdriver, sending waves of disruptive energy into the swirling mass. The chamber trembled violently as the core began to destabilize.

"Time to go!" the Doctor shouted, retreating as the core erupted in a blinding explosion of light.

Back on Gallifrey, the skies cleared as the Dalek fleet fell into disarray. With the symbiotic connection severed, the corrupted Daleks crumbled, their shells collapsing under their own weight.

The Doctor stood on the steps of the Citadel, watching as the last remnants of the Dalek threat faded. Beside him, Venom stirred quietly.

"*We did it,*" Venom said.

The Doctor nodded, a small smile tugging at his lips. "Yes, we did. Together."

For the first time in ages, Gallifrey stood victorious. But the Doctor knew the battle was only part of a larger war—and with Venom by his side, he was ready for whatever came next.

Chapter 17: The Symbiotic Paradox

The TARDIS swirled through the Time Vortex, its engines groaning louder than usual, as though protesting the strain of holding itself together. Inside, the Doctor stood at the console, his face pale and tense as he studied the swirling displays of temporal readings. Numbers flickered and pulsed erratically, and the central column hissed with steam.

"Not good," the Doctor muttered, his fingers flying across the controls. "Definitely not good."

"*What is it?*" Venom's voice echoed in his mind, laced with both concern and curiosity.

The Doctor stopped and turned to face the empty air, his eyes narrowing. "What is it? I'll tell you what it is—it's you. Your absorption of my regeneration energy has destabilized the timeline. You've created a paradox, Venom!"

"*Explain,*" Venom said, its tone calm but firm.

The Doctor ran a hand through his hair, pacing. "Time isn't just linear—it's interwoven, like a tapestry. Regeneration energy is tied to me, to my existence as a Time Lord. When you absorbed it, you created an anomaly—a ripple that's unraveling the threads of time itself. Past, present, future—they're collapsing in on one another!"

"*And the result?*" Venom asked.

The Doctor pointed to the console, where a holographic projection displayed a chaotic swirl of collapsing events. "That. The entirety of existence imploding into a singularity. No more time. No more space. Just... nothing."

"*Then we must act,*" Venom said, its voice resolute. "*Tell me what to do.*"

The Doctor sighed, leaning against the console. "We need to stabilize the paradox before it reaches a critical point. To do that, we have to isolate the exact moment you absorbed the regeneration energy and contain its effects within a temporal buffer."

"And how do we achieve that?"

The Doctor's face darkened. "We go back to the beginning. To the moment you bonded with me."

The TARDIS materialized on the desolate surface of Klyntar, the symbiote homeworld. The skies were a roiling mass of dark clouds, and the ground pulsed faintly with the living energy of the planet. The Doctor stepped out, his coat billowing in the wind, Venom's presence a steady weight in his mind.

"This is where it all started," the Doctor said, his voice low. "The bond. The absorption. The paradox."

"It feels... familiar," Venom said, its tone contemplative. *"Yet wrong. The paradox is here."*

The Doctor nodded, pulling out his sonic screwdriver and scanning the surroundings. The readings were chaotic, the air thick with temporal distortions.

"Time is already breaking down," he said grimly. "We don't have much time."

As they moved through the barren landscape, the distortions became more pronounced. Fragments of other times flickered into view: shadowy figures from the past, bursts of energy from future battles. At one point, a version of the Doctor himself appeared briefly, his face drawn and aged.

"That's... unsettling," the Doctor muttered, shaking his head. "We're walking through echoes of what was and what might be."

"And what must not be," Venom added.

Ahead, a massive temporal rift glowed ominously, its edges crackling with raw energy. Within it, the moment of their first bond replayed in an endless loop: Venom, desperate to survive, reaching out to the Doctor; the Doctor, sacrificing a portion of his regeneration energy to save both of them.

"That's it," the Doctor said, pointing to the rift. "The anchor point. The moment the paradox was born."

"What must we do?" Venom asked.

The Doctor turned to face the rift, his jaw set. "We have to enter the rift and isolate the moment. I'll create a temporal buffer to contain the paradox, but it'll require both of us working together. You'll need to stabilize the bond from within while I manipulate the timeline from outside."

"*It will be dangerous,*" Venom said, a hint of hesitation in its voice. "*For both of us.*"

"Dangerous is what I do," the Doctor replied with a small, wry smile. "Let's get on with it."

Inside the rift, time itself was a maelstrom of swirling energy. The Doctor and Venom stepped into the chaotic vortex, their combined form flickering as the temporal currents buffeted them.

The scene of their first bond loomed ahead, frozen and glowing with an eerie light. The Doctor raised his sonic screwdriver, the device buzzing as he began constructing the temporal buffer.

"Venom, focus on the bond," the Doctor said, his voice strained. "Stabilize it. You have to isolate the energy you absorbed and feed it back into the timeline."

"*Understood,*" Venom said, its voice steady despite the chaos.

The process was grueling. The Doctor worked frantically, his hands a blur as he adjusted the settings on his sonic screwdriver. Venom, meanwhile, concentrated on its connection to the Doctor, delving deep into the bond to find the fragments of regeneration energy it had absorbed.

"*I see it,*" Venom said after a moment. "*The energy is... alive. It resists me.*"

"Of course it resists!" the Doctor shouted over the roar of the rift. "It's tied to me, to my very existence. But you have to push through. Trust me, Venom."

"*I do,*" Venom said, its voice filled with resolve.

With a final surge of effort, Venom reached the core of the energy and began channeling it back into the temporal fabric. The rift trembled violently as the paradox fought back, its chaotic energy lashing out in all directions.

"Hold on!" the Doctor yelled, gripping the sonic screwdriver tightly. "We're almost there!"

At last, the temporal buffer snapped into place, sealing the paradox within a contained loop. The rift's energy subsided, and the chaotic currents of time began to settle.

The Doctor and Venom stood at the heart of the rift, their combined form glowing faintly with residual energy. The Doctor let out a shaky breath, his shoulders slumping with exhaustion.

"We did it," he said softly. "The timeline is stabilizing."

"*The bond is intact,*" Venom said. "*And the paradox is no more.*"

The Doctor smiled faintly. "You did well, Venom. Better than well."

"*You trusted me,*" Venom replied. "*And I trusted you.*"

The Doctor nodded, his gaze thoughtful. "That's what partnerships are built on, Venom. Trust."

As they stepped out of the rift and back onto the surface of Klyntar, the Doctor looked up at the dark skies, his hearts lighter than they had been in days.

"Right then," he said, turning toward the TARDIS. "Another paradox averted, another timeline saved. What's next?"

"*Wherever we are needed,*" Venom replied.

With a grin, the Doctor strode toward the TARDIS, ready for the next adventure—whatever it might be.

Chapter 18: Fused Fates

The TARDIS floated in orbit around a dying star, its golden light bathing the console room in an eerie glow. The Doctor stood motionless, staring at the monitor, while Venom's presence hummed in the back of his mind. The war was escalating; the remnants of the symbiote hive, fractured but still dangerous, had allied with a new faction of Daleks, creating chaos across the galaxy.

"We're running out of time," the Doctor murmured, his voice tinged with exhaustion.

"*The hive is relentless,*" Venom replied. "*They will not stop until they consume everything.*"

The Doctor turned sharply, his expression hard. "Then we stop them, Venom. But not as we are now. Every time we fight, it's reactionary—improvised. We need something more."

Venom's voice grew quieter. "*You mean... complete fusion.*"

"Yes," the Doctor said, his tone firm. "You and I, fully integrated. Not just working together, but becoming one. A singular entity with a unified purpose."

"*That level of symbiosis has risks,*" Venom warned. "*Your mind, your identity—it could be lost.*"

The Doctor's gaze softened, and he gave a small, wry smile. "I know. But the universe is at stake, Venom. If we don't do this, there won't be a timeline left to save."

Venom was silent for a moment, then said, "*I trust you, Doctor. Let us begin.*"

The fusion process was unlike anything either had experienced before. The Doctor sat cross-legged on the floor of the TARDIS, his hands resting on his knees, while Venom's tendrils enveloped him in a cocoon of inky blackness. The room glowed faintly as the symbiote's essence merged with the Doctor's very being.

The Doctor's mind opened wide, and he felt Venom's memories flood in—fragmented flashes of countless hosts, battles, survival, and loss. For its part, Venom experienced the Doctor's life in its entirety: the Time War, the pain of loss, the weight of responsibility, and the unyielding hope that drove him forward.

"*So much pain,*" Venom murmured. "*And yet, you endure.*"

"Because that's what it means to be the Doctor," he replied, his voice calm but resolute. "We keep going, no matter what."

The fusion deepened, their thoughts aligning in perfect harmony. Where there had once been two minds working in tandem, there was now one—a singular entity of unparalleled clarity and power. The Doctor-Venom hybrid rose to its feet, the TARDIS humming in recognition of the transformation.

The Doctor's voice echoed with dual tones, rich and resonant. "We are ready."

The battlefield was a nightmare. Daleks enhanced with corrupted symbiotes rampaged across a desolate planet, their beams tearing through everything in their path. The resistance—a ragtag alliance of Time Lords, humanoids, and freed symbiotes—fought valiantly but were being pushed back, their numbers dwindling.

A Dalek Supreme hovered above the carnage, its voice amplified by the symbiotic energy coursing through its shell. "*EXTERMINATE THE RESISTANCE! INFEST ALL WORLDS!*"

Suddenly, the sky darkened as a shimmering vortex appeared above the battlefield. The TARDIS materialized, its doors swinging open to reveal the Doctor-Venom hybrid. They stepped out, their form radiating an aura of power that silenced the chaos below.

"Daleks," the Doctor-Venom spoke, their voice carrying across the battlefield like a thunderclap. "Your reign of terror ends here."

The Dalek Supreme turned, its eyestalk narrowing. "*DOCTOR. YOU ARE NOTHING COMPARED TO THE MIGHT OF THE HIVE!*"

The Doctor-Venom raised a hand, black tendrils coiling around their arm before lashing out with precision. The tendrils struck the Dalek Supreme's symbiotic enhancements, severing its connection to the hive. The Dalek's movements grew erratic as sparks flew from its shell.

"ERROR! ERROR!" the Dalek screeched before collapsing in a heap.

The other Daleks turned their attention to the Doctor-Venom, opening fire in unison. Beams of energy streaked toward them, but they raised a shimmering shield of symbiotic energy, deflecting the attacks effortlessly.

"Your power is stolen," the Doctor-Venom said, their voice calm but commanding. "Ours is earned."

They moved with impossible speed, darting across the battlefield and dismantling the Daleks with surgical precision. Each strike was calculated, each motion fluid. As they fought, they transmitted a pulse of energy that severed the corrupted symbiotes from their Dalek hosts, rendering the machines inert.

The tide of the battle shifted as the resistance rallied behind the Doctor-Venom. Time Lords unleashed coordinated strikes with temporal disruptors, while freed symbiotes worked alongside humanoids to neutralize the remaining Daleks.

Kael, the leader of the resistance, approached the Doctor-Venom amidst the chaos, their expression one of awe. "Doctor, or... Venom... or whatever you are now—what's next?"

The Doctor-Venom turned to Kael, their glowing eyes softening. "This war ends today. The hive's nexus must be destroyed, or their corruption will spread to every corner of the universe."

Kael nodded. "Then we follow you."

The final confrontation took place at the hive's central nexus, a massive structure pulsating with dark energy. The Doctor-Venom led the charge, their presence inspiring the resistance as they pushed through the hive's defenses.

Inside the nexus, the air was thick with symbiotic tendrils that writhed and lashed out like living weapons. At the heart of the chamber stood the hive's core—a swirling mass of energy that radiated malevolence.

"*Doctor,*" the hive spoke, its voice a cacophony of countless voices. "*You cannot destroy us. We are eternal.*"

"No," the Doctor-Venom replied, stepping forward. "You're a parasite. And your time is over."

They raised their hands, channeling their combined energy into a focused pulse. The core trembled, its tendrils flailing wildly as it fought back. The resistance held the line, fending off waves of corrupted symbiotes while the Doctor-Venom concentrated on dismantling the hive's connection to the universe.

"Venom," the Doctor said internally, their thoughts perfectly aligned. "This is it. Let's finish this."

"*Together,*" Venom replied.

With a final surge of power, the Doctor-Venom unleashed a blinding wave of energy that engulfed the core. The nexus collapsed in on itself, its tendrils disintegrating as the hive's presence was erased from existence.

As the dust settled, the battlefield fell silent. The remaining Daleks and corrupted symbiotes lay lifeless, their connection to the hive severed. The resistance stood victorious, though the cost had been high.

The Doctor-Venom stood at the heart of the ruins, their form flickering as they began to separate. The tendrils receded, and the Doctor emerged, his face pale but determined.

"Venom," he said softly. "We did it."

"*Yes,*" Venom replied, its voice faint but content. "*Thank you, Doctor. For showing me a better way.*"

The Doctor smiled faintly. "Freedom, Venom. It's messy, but it's worth it."

As the TARDIS dematerialized, the Doctor looked out at the stars, his hearts heavy but hopeful. The war was over, but the universe still had much healing to do—and he would be there to help, no matter the cost.

Chapter 19: The Hive's Ultimate Weapon

The TARDIS materialized on a desolate moon orbiting a dying star. The landscape was a wasteland of jagged rocks and swirling dust storms, the perfect hiding place for something the universe was never meant to see. Inside, the Doctor's face was grim as he adjusted the controls, the hum of the engines unusually strained.

Venom's voice echoed in his mind, tinged with concern. *"Doctor, this place... it feels wrong. The air, the ground, even the stars—they vibrate with unease."*

The Doctor nodded, his eyes fixed on the monitor displaying energy readings that spiked off the charts. "That's because something unnatural is here, Venom. Something big. And it's waiting for us."

"The hive's last weapon," Venom said, its tone growing darker. *"A monstrosity born of desperation."*

The Doctor adjusted his coat and took a deep breath. "Then it's time we introduced ourselves."

The Doctor stepped out of the TARDIS, his boots crunching against the cracked surface of the moon. The air was heavy, charged with an oppressive energy that seemed to press down on him. Venom's presence coiled protectively around him, a steady reassurance in the foreboding silence.

As they approached the source of the energy readings, the ground began to tremble. A low, mechanical growl rumbled through the air, growing louder with each step. The Doctor stopped abruptly as a massive shadow emerged from the swirling dust—a towering figure that defied reason.

The creature was a horrifying amalgamation of symbiotic fluid and Dalek technology. Its body was a grotesque blend of organic tendrils and metal plating, with glowing red lights pulsating across its surface. Its eyestalk, now fused with a swirling mass of symbiote energy, glowed like a malevolent star.

The creature's voice boomed, an unholy fusion of Dalek rage and symbiotic malice. "*I AM PERFECTION. THE ULTIMATE HYBRID. I AM THE END OF ALL THINGS.*"

The Doctor tilted his head, his expression a mixture of fascination and horror. "Well, you're certainly not winning any beauty contests."

"*DOCTOR,*" the creature roared, its voice shaking the ground. "*YOUR RESISTANCE IS FUTILE. THE UNIVERSE WILL FALL.*"

The Doctor smirked, his hands slipping into his coat pockets. "Oh, I've heard that one before. Spoiler alert: it never ends well for the ones who say it."

"*Be wary,*" Venom whispered. "*This creature is unlike anything we've faced. Its power rivals ours.*"

The Doctor's smirk faded. "Noted."

The battle began with an earth-shattering roar as the hybrid unleashed a barrage of tendrils and energy blasts. The Doctor darted to the side, his movements enhanced by Venom's agility. He raised his sonic screwdriver, sending a high-frequency pulse that disrupted the hybrid's symbiotic tendrils, but only for a moment.

The creature retaliated with a swipe of its massive, claw-like appendage, forcing the Doctor to roll out of the way. As he regained his footing, he muttered, "This thing is faster than it looks."

"*And stronger,*" Venom added, its voice strained. "*Its connection to the hive enhances its abilities.*"

The Doctor narrowed his eyes. "Then we need to sever that connection."

The hybrid charged, its massive frame tearing through the landscape like a living battering ram. The Doctor leapt onto a nearby ledge, narrowly avoiding the impact as Venom's tendrils lashed out to anchor him.

"Venom, can you sense the core?" the Doctor asked, his voice urgent.

"*Yes,*" Venom replied. "*It is buried deep within its body, a fusion of Dalek technology and symbiotic essence. But it is heavily shielded.*"

The Doctor's mind raced. "If we disrupt the Dalek components, it'll destabilize the core. We just need a way in."

"*I can create an opening,*" Venom said. "*But it will leave us vulnerable.*"

The Doctor hesitated for only a moment. "Do it. We don't have a choice."

Venom surged through the Doctor, black tendrils wrapping around his arms and forming sharp, claw-like extensions. The hybrid roared as Venom struck with precision, slicing through its outer defenses and exposing a pulsating mass of energy beneath its armor.

The Doctor seized the opportunity, leaping onto the creature's back and using his sonic screwdriver to emit a pulse directly into the exposed core. The hybrid convulsed, its movements growing erratic as sparks flew from its body.

"*You cannot defeat me!*" the hybrid bellowed, its voice distorted with rage. "*I AM IMMORTAL!*"

The Doctor gritted his teeth, clinging to the thrashing creature. "Immortal, maybe. Unstoppable? Let's test that theory."

The hybrid retaliated with a surge of energy, throwing the Doctor off its back. He landed hard, coughing as he scrambled to his feet. Venom's presence steadied him, their combined strength keeping him upright.

"*Doctor,*" Venom said, its voice urgent. "*The core is unstable. One more strike will destroy it—but it will also release a massive energy wave.*"

The Doctor's expression hardened. "And that wave will wipe out everything on this moon, including us."

"*Correct,*" Venom replied.

The Doctor's lips curled into a grim smile. "Then we make sure it's worth it."

The hybrid prepared for another attack, its massive frame glowing with destructive energy. The Doctor stood his ground, his sonic screwdriver in one hand and Venom's tendrils coiled around the other.

"Hey!" the Doctor called, his voice cutting through the chaos. "Didn't anyone tell you? Daleks make terrible hosts!"

The hybrid roared, charging forward with all its might. The Doctor and Venom moved as one, their combined strength and agility allowing them to dodge the attack and strike at the core with a final, devastating blow.

The hybrid let out a deafening scream as its core shattered, releasing a blinding wave of energy that engulfed the entire moon.

When the light faded, the Doctor found himself lying on the cracked ground, his body aching but intact. Venom's presence was faint but steady, a quiet reassurance in the aftermath of the battle.

"Venom?" the Doctor whispered.

"*I am here,*" Venom replied, its voice weak but determined. "*We survived.*"

The Doctor let out a shaky laugh, his head falling back against the ground. "Barely."

As he struggled to his feet, he looked around at the devastated landscape. The hybrid was gone, its remains reduced to smoldering debris. The war wasn't over, but its greatest threat had been neutralized.

The Doctor gazed up at the stars, his hearts heavy but resolute. "One battle at a time, Venom. One battle at a time."

Chapter 20: A Symbiotic Sacrifice

The TARDIS hummed softly as it floated in the middle of a dying galaxy, its light dimmed against the backdrop of collapsing stars. Inside, the Doctor stood at the console, his hands gripping its edges tightly. His face was lined with exhaustion, his usual boundless energy tempered by the weight of the war. Across from him, Venom's presence swirled restlessly, coiling around his mind like a storm.

"*The hive's core remains,*" Venom said quietly. "*As long as it exists, this war will never end.*"

The Doctor nodded, his expression grim. "I know. It's always about the core, isn't it? The beating heart of the enemy, protected by layers of destruction. But this one... this one's different. It's not just a physical place—it's a psychic nexus, holding the hive together."

"*And there is only one way to destroy it,*" Venom replied. "*I must sever the connection myself. Completely.*"

The Doctor's head snapped up, his eyes narrowing. "No. Absolutely not."

"*Doctor,*" Venom said, its tone uncharacteristically gentle. "*You know it's the only way. My connection to the hive is the key. If I return to the core, I can destroy it from within.*"

The Doctor slammed his hand against the console. "And what happens to you, Venom? You're destroyed along with it? I won't allow that."

"*My purpose has always been survival,*" Venom said. "*But now, I understand there are greater purposes than mine.*"

The Doctor's voice rose, filled with frustration and grief. "You don't get to make that choice alone. We've come too far, Venom. We've fought too hard. There has to be another way."

The TARDIS landed in the heart of a lifeless planet, its surface scorched and barren, riddled with massive fissures that pulsed faintly with a dark energy. This was the hive's last stronghold, its psychic core buried deep within the planet's crust. The Doctor stepped out, his coat flaring in the oppressive wind, his face set with determination.

"Here we are," he said quietly. "Ground zero."

"*This place reeks of death,*" Venom said, its voice low. "*The hive's power has corrupted even the soil.*"

The Doctor adjusted his sonic screwdriver, scanning the area. "And if we don't stop it, that corruption spreads to the rest of the universe."

As they moved toward the fissures, the ground trembled, and massive tendrils erupted from below, writhing like serpents. The Doctor leapt back, narrowly avoiding a strike.

"Ah, they know we're here," he muttered. "That's never a good sign."

"*They are afraid,*" Venom said. "*They know I am coming.*"

Deeper inside the planet, the psychic core loomed ahead—a massive, pulsating orb of black and red energy, suspended in the air by tendrils that writhed like veins. It radiated an oppressive energy that made the Doctor's hearts pound in his chest.

"*Doctor,*" Venom said, its voice quieter now. "*This is where it ends. Let me go.*"

The Doctor stared at the core, his jaw tightening. "No. Not like this. You said it yourself, Venom—you've learned what it means to have a purpose beyond survival. But that purpose isn't sacrifice. Not if I can help it."

"*You have a plan,*" Venom observed. "*You always do.*"

The Doctor's lips curled into a faint smile. "You're catching on."

He turned back toward the TARDIS, his mind racing. "The core is a psychic nexus, right? It's connected to every symbiote in the hive. If we flood it with an opposing signal, something strong enough to disrupt its resonance, we could sever its hold on every host."

"*That would require immense energy,*" Venom said. "*More than even the hive possesses.*"

The Doctor's gaze hardened. "The TARDIS has the energy we need. Its telepathic circuits can amplify the signal and create a wave strong enough to break the hive's control."

"*And the risk?*" Venom asked.

The Doctor hesitated, his voice softening. "The wave could destabilize the core completely. There's a chance the entire planet—and us along with it—will be obliterated."

"*A small price for freedom,*" Venom said. "*I trust you, Doctor.*"

Back inside the TARDIS, the Doctor worked frantically, connecting the telepathic circuits to the central console. The room pulsed with a growing energy as the ship's engines roared to life.

"Come on, old girl," the Doctor murmured, his hands flying over the controls. "Just a little more. You've got this."

"*Doctor,*" Venom said, its voice steady. "*If this fails—*"

"It won't," the Doctor interrupted, his tone resolute. "We don't fail, Venom. Not when it matters."

The TARDIS shuddered violently as the energy built to a crescendo. The console sparked, and the central column pulsed with a brilliant light.

"*It's ready,*" Venom said.

The Doctor nodded, placing his hands on the console. "Then let's do this."

The TARDIS unleashed a wave of pure, telepathic energy, surging through the fissures and into the hive's core. The psychic tendrils writhed in agony as the core's energy flickered and dimmed.

Outside, across the universe, symbiotes began to recoil, their connection to the hive severed. Hosts fell to the ground, their bodies freed from the hive's control. The war was ending.

But the core fought back, its energy flaring with a desperate intensity. The planet trembled, and cracks spread across its surface.

"Doctor!" Venom warned. "*The core is collapsing!*"

The Doctor gripped the console, his face illuminated by the pulsing light. "Hold on, Venom. Just a little longer!"

With a final surge of energy, the core imploded, its remnants disintegrating into nothingness. The TARDIS rocked violently, its systems straining against the backlash. But then, as quickly as it had started, the chaos subsided.

When the Doctor opened his eyes, the TARDIS was silent. The central console hummed faintly, its light dim but steady. He slumped against the controls, his body trembling with exhaustion.

"Venom?" he whispered.

"*I am here,*" Venom replied, its voice softer than he'd ever heard it. "*We succeeded. The hive is gone.*"

The Doctor let out a shaky laugh, his head falling back against the console. "We did it. We actually did it."

"*The hosts are free,*" Venom said. "*And so am I.*"

The Doctor smiled faintly. "Freedom, Venom. It's a messy thing. But it's worth it."

As the TARDIS drifted through the quiet void, the Doctor allowed himself a moment of peace, knowing that, for the first time in a long time, the universe was just a little bit safer.

Chapter 21: The Rebirth of Gallifrey

The spires of Gallifrey gleamed in the twin suns' light once more, though scars from the war remained etched across the Capitol and its surrounding landscapes. Craters from battles marred the terrain, and faint traces of symbiotic corruption lingered in the air. Inside the Citadel, Time Lords bustled about, their ornate robes flowing as they worked to restore their society.

The Doctor stood at the heart of the High Council chamber, his hands tucked into his coat pockets. His usual easy grin was absent, replaced by a wary expression as he faced the gathered Council. Venom's presence was quiet but constant, a subtle hum in the back of his mind.

Rassilon, seated at the head of the chamber, surveyed the Doctor with a mixture of disdain and grudging respect. "Doctor," he began, his voice cold but steady. "Gallifrey owes its survival to you. But your methods... they raise questions."

The Doctor raised an eyebrow. "Oh, do they now? Is this the part where you thank me with one hand and wag your finger at me with the other?"

"You allied with a symbiote," Rassilon said, his tone sharp. "A creature born of the hive that nearly destroyed us. Some might call that betrayal."

The Doctor took a step forward, his voice calm but firm. "And some might call it survival. Venom chose freedom, Rassilon. It fought against the hive, just like we did. Without it, Gallifrey wouldn't be here to argue about this."

Murmurs rippled through the Council chamber, some Time Lords nodding in agreement while others frowned in disapproval. One elder, his face lined with age and wisdom, stood. "Doctor, no one denies your role in our survival. But the question remains—can we trust this... Venom?"

"*I am here,*" Venom said, its voice echoing through the chamber, causing several Time Lords to flinch. "*And I fight for freedom, not domination.*"

The Doctor smirked, spreading his arms. "See? Venom's perfectly capable of speaking for itself."

"That is precisely what concerns us," another Council member said, his tone wary. "A symbiote with autonomy is unprecedented. It could pose a threat."

The Doctor's eyes hardened. "So could every decision you make, every time you meddle with the universe. Shall we start questioning your autonomy, too?"

The chamber fell silent, the weight of his words settling over the gathered Time Lords. Rassilon's expression darkened, but he held his tongue.

After the meeting, the Doctor walked through the Citadel's reconstructed halls, his mind heavy with the tension from the Council. The scars of the war were everywhere—cracked walls, dimmed lights, and faces etched with weariness.

"*They fear me,*" Venom said, its tone contemplative. "*And they fear you for accepting me.*"

The Doctor sighed. "They fear what they don't understand, Venom. They always have. Time Lords are brilliant, but their arrogance blinds them."

"*And you?*" Venom asked. "*Do you fear me?*"

The Doctor stopped, leaning against a balcony railing that overlooked the Capitol. He gazed out at the city, his voice soft. "I did. At first. But fear isn't always a bad thing. It keeps you cautious, makes you question your choices. And when you push through it, you find something stronger."

"*Trust,*" Venom said, its voice quieter now.

The Doctor nodded. "Exactly."

Later that day, the Doctor found himself in the Capitol's plaza, surrounded by survivors of the war—Time Lords, symbiote hosts who had been freed, and other allies who had fought to save Gallifrey. A makeshift stage had been set up, and Rassilon himself stood at the forefront, addressing the gathered crowd.

"Today, we stand as survivors," Rassilon proclaimed, his voice carrying across the plaza. "Gallifrey has endured trials that would have destroyed lesser civilizations. We owe our survival to the courage and sacrifice of many—but one stands out above the rest."

The Doctor shifted uncomfortably as all eyes turned to him. Rassilon gestured for him to step forward, and he reluctantly climbed onto the stage.

"Doctor," Rassilon continued, his tone begrudging but genuine. "Your actions, though unconventional, saved Gallifrey. For that, we honor you."

The crowd erupted into applause, though it was tinged with a mix of admiration and uncertainty. The Doctor raised a hand, silencing the cheers.

"Thank you," he said, his voice steady but firm. "But let's be clear—this wasn't just me. This was all of us. Time Lords, humans, freed symbiotes... even Venom."

He paused, letting the name hang in the air. "Yes, Venom. The so-called monster you fear. The creature that chose to fight for freedom when it could have chosen destruction. If there's one thing this war has taught me, it's that redemption isn't just possible—it's essential. And if Venom can choose a better path, so can we."

The crowd murmured, and the Doctor scanned their faces. Some looked thoughtful, others skeptical, but a few nodded in agreement.

"The universe is full of second chances," the Doctor concluded. "Gallifrey doesn't just need to recover—it needs to change. And that starts with understanding, not fear."

As the crowd dispersed, Kael, the leader of the resistance, approached the Doctor. Their face was lined with battle scars, but their eyes shone with respect.

"Doctor," Kael said, offering a hand. "That was... inspiring. You've given us more than just survival—you've given us hope."

The Doctor shook their hand, a small smile tugging at his lips. "Hope's a powerful thing, Kael. Don't let go of it."

Kael hesitated, then added, "And Venom... it's lucky to have you. You make a good team."

The Doctor chuckled softly. "Don't let it hear you say that. It'll get a big head."

"*Too late,*" Venom said, its voice laced with amusement.

That evening, the Doctor stood on the steps of the TARDIS, gazing out at the Capitol as its lights flickered back to life. The city was rebuilding, and so was its people. But there was still a long road ahead.

"*You could stay,*" Venom said. "*Help them rebuild.*"

The Doctor shook his head. "Gallifrey doesn't need me, Venom. Not anymore. They need to find their own way."

"*And you?*" Venom asked. "*What do you need?*"

The Doctor smiled faintly, stepping into the TARDIS. "Oh, you know me. I need the stars."

As the TARDIS dematerialized, the Doctor felt a quiet sense of resolution. Gallifrey was healing, and the universe was safe—for now. And with Venom by his side, he was ready for whatever came next. Together, they were more than a Time Lord and a symbiote.

They were something new. Something better. And their journey was far from over.

Chapter 22: Symbiote Diplomacy

The TARDIS hummed softly as it materialized on the lush plains of Veridian IV, a neutral planet known for hosting intergalactic summits. Its golden grass shimmered in the light of two suns, and the air was alive with the sounds of alien fauna. It was a peaceful place—a stark contrast to the tension the Doctor knew awaited him inside the summit chamber.

As the Doctor stepped out of the TARDIS, Venom's voice echoed in his mind. "*This place is strange... calm. It feels wrong to hold such heavy matters here.*"

"Peace is the best starting point for a treaty, Venom," the Doctor replied, straightening his coat. "Though, I'll admit, getting the galaxy to accept symbiotes as anything but enemies is a tall order."

"*They fear us,*" Venom said simply. "*And they should.*"

The Doctor stopped, glancing toward the summit building—a gleaming structure made of crystal and steel. "Fear is the easy choice. Understanding? That's the hard part. But it's possible. I've seen it."

"*Do you truly believe they will listen?*" Venom asked, its tone skeptical.

The Doctor smiled faintly. "They'll listen to me. And if they don't, they'll definitely listen to you."

Inside the summit chamber, representatives from dozens of species had gathered. The air buzzed with heated debate, their voices overlapping as accusations and defenses flew back and forth.

"The symbiotes nearly destroyed entire star systems!" a Rigellian delegate shouted, their tentacles waving angrily. "How can we trust them now?"

"They were under the control of the hive," countered a humanoid representative from Vareshka Prime, one of the few worlds that had learned to coexist with symbiotes. "The hive is gone. They deserve a chance to prove themselves."

The Doctor entered the chamber, his presence immediately drawing attention. The din quieted as all eyes turned to him. He strode to the center of the room, his hands tucked into his coat pockets, and surveyed the gathered crowd.

"Hello!" he said brightly, breaking the tension. "I'm the Doctor, and I'm here to stop you all from making a terrible mistake."

The Rigellian delegate scowled. "What mistake would that be, Doctor?"

The Doctor's expression turned serious. "The mistake of judging an entire species based on fear. Yes, the symbiotes have caused harm—terrible harm. But they've also been enslaved, manipulated, and misunderstood. The hive is gone now, and with it, the force that drove them to war. What's left is a species searching for its place in the universe."

"And what place would that be?" asked a reptilian delegate, their voice hissing. "As parasites? Predators?"

The Doctor's eyes narrowed. "No. As equals."

Venom stirred within the Doctor, then began to manifest, black tendrils coiling around his arms as it stepped forward, forming its sleek, armored shape. The room tensed, and several delegates recoiled in fear. Venom's white eyes scanned the crowd, its voice calm but resonant.

"*You fear me,*" Venom said. "*I understand why. For centuries, my kind have been tools of destruction. But that is not who we are. Not anymore.*"

"Why should we believe you?" the Rigellian delegate snapped.

Venom paused, glancing at the Doctor. "*Because I chose a better path. I fought against the hive. I fought for freedom—not just for myself, but for all symbiotes. And I am here now, not as an enemy, but as an ambassador.*"

The Doctor stepped forward, his voice steady. "Venom represents what's possible. Redemption, growth, and coexistence. But this won't work if only one side is willing to change. If the universe treats the symbiotes as monsters, they'll have no choice but to act like monsters. Give them a chance, and you'll see what they can become."

The Vareshkan representative stood. "We have already seen it. On Vareshka Prime, symbiotes and hosts live in harmony. They protect us, and we offer them companionship and purpose. It is a partnership, not an infestation."

The room murmured with surprise, and a few delegates exchanged thoughtful glances.

After hours of debate, a tentative agreement was reached. The galaxy would recognize symbiotes as a sentient species with the right to exist peacefully. A council would be formed to oversee their integration, and Venom was appointed as their ambassador.

As the delegates dispersed, the Doctor and Venom stood together outside the chamber, the twin suns casting long shadows across the plains.

"*They agreed,*" Venom said, its voice filled with a mix of awe and uncertainty. "*But will they honor their word?*"

"They will," the Doctor replied. "Because you'll hold them to it. You'll show them what symbiotes are capable of."

"*I learned that from you,*" Venom said quietly. "*You trusted me when no one else would. You showed me a better way.*"

The Doctor smiled, his eyes glinting with pride. "And now you'll show the universe. You've come a long way, Venom."

"*Thanks to you,*" Venom replied. "*But our journey isn't over. Not yet.*"

The Doctor glanced at the TARDIS, its familiar shape standing against the horizon. "No, it isn't. There's always more to do."

As Venom stepped forward, the Doctor lingered for a moment, looking out at the alien plains. The universe had taken its first step toward understanding—and perhaps, just perhaps, it was a step toward something greater.

"Right then," the Doctor said, turning back to the TARDIS. "Let's see where the stars take us next."

Chapter 23: A New Universe

The TARDIS hummed softly as it landed on Klyntar, the symbiote homeworld. But this time, the planet felt different. No longer shrouded in the oppressive energy of the hive, its skies were clearer, its surface alive with strange bioluminescent flora and fauna. The air hummed with the promise of renewal.

The Doctor stepped out, his coat flaring in the gentle breeze, his expression a mix of curiosity and cautious optimism. Venom coiled protectively within him, its presence calm but contemplative.

"*Home,*" Venom said softly. "*But not as I remember it.*"

The Doctor looked around, his sonic screwdriver buzzing faintly as he scanned the area. "It's a fresh start, Venom. The hive's gone, and this planet has a chance to become something new. Something better."

"*If we can protect it,*" Venom replied. "*The scars of the hive run deep.*"

The Doctor nodded, his expression serious. "Scars heal, but they leave marks. It's how you grow from them that matters."

The pair made their way to the heart of Klyntar, a sprawling city built of organic material that pulsed faintly with life. Freed symbiotes moved through the streets, their forms shifting fluidly as they interacted with one another and their newly liberated environment. Some merged with local fauna, forming symbiotic partnerships that seemed natural and harmonious.

As they walked, a small group of symbiotes approached, their forms coalescing into humanoid shapes. One of them, taller and more defined than the rest, stepped forward. Its voice was deep and resonant, carrying an air of authority.

"*You are Venom,*" it said, inclining its head. "*The one who broke the hive's chains.*"

Venom stirred within the Doctor, stepping forward to take its own form. Its black, sleek body gleamed in the planet's light, its white eyes glowing softly.

"*I am,*" Venom said. "*But I did not do it alone. This is the Doctor. Without him, I would still be enslaved.*"

The symbiote leader turned its gaze to the Doctor, who gave a small wave. "Hello! Just passing through, really. Thought we'd see how the neighborhood's doing."

"*It is... recovering,*" the leader said. "*But there is much to rebuild. The hive's presence lingers in our memories, and many of our kind do not know how to live without it.*"

The Doctor tilted his head, his tone softening. "Freedom's a tricky thing. It's messy and confusing, especially when you've never had it before. But it's also full of possibility."

"*And danger,*" Venom added.

The leader nodded. "*Yes. We have sensed disturbances in the skies beyond our world. Shadows that do not belong.*"

The Doctor and Venom were escorted to the city's central structure, a massive organic tower that pulsated faintly with light. Inside, symbiote elders gathered around a bioluminescent map of the stars. Tendrils of light traced constellations and planetary systems, highlighting areas of concern.

One of the elders spoke, its voice soft but urgent. "*Since the hive's fall, we have noticed anomalies in the stars. Shifts in gravitational patterns, bursts of energy unlike anything we have seen.*"

The Doctor leaned in, his brow furrowed as he studied the map. "Anomalies, you say? Could be natural, but... given everything we've been through, I'm guessing it's not."

"*It feels wrong,*" Venom said. "*Like something is watching.*"

The Doctor straightened, his eyes sharp. "Watching? That's not ominous at all."

One of the younger symbiotes, its form flickering nervously, stepped forward. "*There have been... sightings. Strange shapes in the void. They do not approach, but they linger.*"

The Doctor's jaw tightened. "Lingering shadows. Could be a remnant of the hive's psychic influence—or something entirely new."

The Doctor and Venom decided to investigate, traveling to the edge of Klyntar's system where the disturbances had been reported. The TARDIS materialized on a rocky moon, its surface bathed in the light of distant stars. The air was thin, the landscape barren and cold.

The Doctor stepped out, his sonic screwdriver buzzing as he scanned the area. "Something's definitely off," he muttered. "Energy readings are spiking, but there's no source. It's like..."

"*Like the void is alive,*" Venom finished, its voice tense.

Suddenly, the ground trembled, and a fissure split the rocky surface. From the crack emerged a swirling mass of shadow and light, its form shifting and writhing as it loomed before them. The Doctor took a step back, his expression a mix of awe and caution.

"Well, that's new," he said. "Hello there! I'm the Doctor, and this is Venom. Care to introduce yourself?"

The entity didn't respond with words, but a wave of energy surged toward them, forcing the Doctor to dive out of the way. Venom reacted instantly, enveloping the Doctor in its sleek armor and shielding him from the blast.

"*Hostile,*" Venom said, its tone grim. "*It feels... ancient.*"

The Doctor's mind raced as he activated his sonic screwdriver, emitting a pulse that disrupted the entity's form for a brief moment. "It's not hive-related," he muttered. "This is something else entirely."

The entity recoiled, its shadowy tendrils retreating slightly before lashing out again. The Doctor and Venom moved as one, dodging and countering with precision. But the creature's power was immense, its attacks relentless.

"Venom!" the Doctor shouted. "Can you sense anything? A weakness?"

"*It is not a creature,*" Venom said. "*It is... a force. A fragment of something larger.*"

The Doctor's eyes widened. "A fragment? Of what?"

Before Venom could answer, the entity suddenly dissipated, vanishing into the void as quickly as it had appeared. The ground grew still, the air heavy with an unsettling silence.

"*It is gone,*" Venom said. "*But it will return.*"

The Doctor frowned, his gaze fixed on the stars. "And when it does, we'll be ready."

Back on Klyntar, the Doctor and Venom shared their findings with the symbiote leaders. The news was met with concern, but also determination.

"*We have faced the hive and survived,*" the leader said. "*We will face this new threat as well.*"

The Doctor nodded. "Good. Because whatever's out there, it's not just coming for you. It's coming for all of us."

As the TARDIS prepared to leave, Venom lingered for a moment, its gaze fixed on the horizon. "*This world is changing,*" it said. "*We are changing.*"

The Doctor placed a hand on the console, his voice soft. "Change is the universe's way of moving forward, Venom. And you're a part of that now."

"*Thanks to you,*" Venom replied.

The Doctor smiled faintly. "Thanks to us."

As the TARDIS dematerialized, the stars seemed to shimmer with a new light—a reminder that even in the face of the unknown, hope and courage would always shine through. The Doctor and Venom, bound by trust and purpose, were ready for whatever lay ahead. Together, they were more than just travelers.

They were defenders of a new universe.

Chapter 24: The Doctor's Shadow

The TARDIS hummed softly in the Time Vortex, its warm, familiar glow casting long shadows across the console room. The Doctor leaned against the console, his eyes fixed on the swirling vortex displayed on the monitor. His usual frenetic energy was absent, replaced by a quiet stillness that seemed to weigh heavily on him.

Venom stirred within him, its presence a constant hum at the back of his mind. "*You are unsettled,*" it said, its voice low and contemplative. "*This is unlike you.*"

The Doctor sighed, running a hand through his hair. "Unsettled is an understatement, Venom. I've faced Daleks, Cybermen, Weeping Angels, and the end of time itself, but this—this is different."

"*Because it is personal,*" Venom replied. "*You fear what we are becoming.*"

The Doctor turned sharply, his voice tinged with frustration. "Because I don't know what we're becoming! Look at me—I'm not just the Doctor anymore. I'm... something else. Something I don't fully understand."

"*And that frightens you,*" Venom said, its tone calm but probing. "*You are not accustomed to being unsure.*"

The Doctor barked a humorless laugh. "Oh, I'm always unsure. The difference is, I can usually figure things out eventually. But this—this bond between us—it's deeper than anything I've ever experienced. And I don't know if I'll ever be just me again."

The TARDIS landed on a quiet, uncharted moon surrounded by nebulae that shimmered in hues of purple and gold. The Doctor stepped out, his boots crunching softly against the crystalline surface. The air was still, the only sound the faint hum of the TARDIS behind him.

Venom's voice broke the silence. "*You brought us here for a reason.*"

The Doctor nodded, staring out at the endless expanse of stars. "This place... it's a neutral zone. A blank slate. I needed somewhere quiet to think."

"*And to confront me,*" Venom said.

The Doctor hesitated before speaking, his voice quieter now. "Yes. This bond between us—it's changing me, Venom. I can feel it. My thoughts, my instincts—they're not entirely my own anymore. And I know you feel it too."

Venom didn't respond immediately, but the air seemed to grow heavier, as if it were considering the Doctor's words. Finally, it said, "*I have noticed the changes. Your resilience, your resourcefulness... they have shaped me as well. But this bond was forged in necessity. Survival. It was never meant to last.*"

The Doctor turned, his gaze sharp. "And yet it has. We've become something new—something neither of us fully understands. And now I have to ask myself: can we ever separate? Should we?"

"*Would you want to?*" Venom asked, its voice softer now.

The question caught the Doctor off guard. He paused, his thoughts swirling. "I don't know," he admitted. "That's the problem, Venom. I don't know who I am anymore."

As they walked across the moon's surface, the Doctor found himself speaking more freely, his thoughts spilling out like a torrent.

"You know, I've spent centuries defining myself. The Doctor. The man who saves people. The last of the Time Lords. But now... now I'm something else. Something more—and less—than what I was. And it scares me."

"*You fear losing your identity,*" Venom said. "*But you have not lost it. You have shared it. As have I.*"

The Doctor stopped, turning to face the horizon. "But where does one end and the other begin? When I make a decision, is it mine? Or ours?"

Venom hesitated, then said, "*Perhaps there is no longer a difference. Perhaps that is what symbiosis truly means.*"

The Doctor frowned, his brow furrowing. "Symbiosis... It's not just about survival, is it? It's about unity. But unity doesn't mean losing yourself."

"*No,*" Venom agreed. "*Unity is balance. It is understanding. I do not seek to consume you, Doctor. I seek to coexist.*"

The Doctor let out a long breath, his shoulders relaxing slightly. "Coexistence. That's the tricky part, isn't it? Learning to live together without losing what makes us... us."

As they returned to the TARDIS, the Doctor leaned against the console, his expression thoughtful. "Venom, if we were to separate—if it were possible—what would happen to you?"

"*I do not know,*" Venom admitted. "*Without the hive, I am... incomplete. But I would survive. I always do.*"

The Doctor tilted his head. "And me? Would I be the same person I was before we met?"

"*No,*" Venom said without hesitation. "*You have changed, Doctor. Just as I have. The bond has shaped us both. To undo it would be to lose what we have become.*"

The Doctor was silent for a long moment, his mind racing. Finally, he said, "Then maybe separation isn't the answer. Maybe the answer is learning to accept what we are now—together."

"*Acceptance is not weakness,*" Venom said. "*It is strength.*"

The Doctor smiled faintly. "You're starting to sound like me."

"*Perhaps you are starting to sound like me,*" Venom replied, its tone tinged with amusement.

As the TARDIS re-entered the Time Vortex, the Doctor felt a strange sense of peace settle over him. The questions hadn't all been answered, and the future was as uncertain as ever. But for now, he and Venom were aligned, their bond a fragile but growing harmony.

"Right then," the Doctor said, flipping a lever. "Where to next?"

"*Somewhere we are needed,*" Venom replied.

The Doctor grinned. "Always. Let's see where the stars take us."

And as the TARDIS roared into the unknown, the Doctor and Venom faced the future—not as separate beings, but as something greater. Together, they were more than Time Lord and symbiote.

They were a shadow and a light, intertwined, ready to face whatever lay ahead.

Chapter 25: Venom Eternal

The TARDIS hummed softly in the Time Vortex, a comforting, familiar sound that filled the console room with its steady rhythm. The Doctor stood at the controls, his coat draped casually over a nearby chair, his expression one of quiet contemplation. Venom's presence was steady, a silent companion within him, as they both processed the journey that had brought them to this moment.

"Doctor," Venom began, its voice a resonant echo in his mind. *"We have faced countless battles, shattered worlds, and saved lives together. Yet I wonder... where do we go from here?"*

The Doctor glanced at the central console, his lips curling into a faint smile. "Anywhere we want, Venom. That's the beauty of the TARDIS, of what we've become. There's no limit to what we can do."

"And yet," Venom said, *"our fusion is unlike anything this universe has ever seen. Do you not fear what we might become?"*

The Doctor turned, leaning against the console as he studied the swirling vortex on the monitor. "Oh, I've been afraid plenty of times, Venom. Fear's just part of the package when you're the Doctor. But here's the thing—fear doesn't stop me. It pushes me forward."

"You have taught me much about pushing forward," Venom admitted. *"About purpose, about freedom. I owe my transformation to you."*

The Doctor chuckled softly, shaking his head. "And I owe mine to you. Funny, isn't it? A Time Lord and a symbiote, of all things, becoming... this."

"It is... unusual," Venom agreed. *"But it is also right."*

The TARDIS materialized on a small, lush planet on the edge of a distant galaxy. Its surface was covered in vibrant forests that glowed faintly in the starlight, and the air hummed with the energy of countless interconnected ecosystems. The Doctor stepped out, his boots crunching softly against the mossy ground.

"Look at this place," he said, spreading his arms wide. "A whole world of wonders, just waiting to be discovered."

"*It is peaceful,*" Venom observed. "*But I sense unrest beneath its surface.*"

The Doctor tilted his head, pulling out his sonic screwdriver and scanning the environment. "Unrest? Hmmm. Let's take a look, shall we?"

As they walked, the Doctor spoke more freely, his thoughts flowing like a stream. "You know, Venom, when we first bonded, I thought it was temporary. Just another strange encounter in a long, strange life. But now, after everything we've been through... I can't imagine being without you."

"*Nor I without you,*" Venom said. "*You have become more than a host. You are a partner, an equal.*"

The Doctor paused, turning to face the horizon. "That's just it, isn't it? We've become something new. Something this universe has never seen before. And maybe that's exactly what the universe needs."

They reached a clearing where a group of alien creatures—small, bioluminescent beings with delicate wings—were gathered around a wounded member of their kind. The Doctor knelt beside the injured creature, his voice soothing as he examined it.

"Don't worry," he murmured. "We'll fix this."

Venom extended a tendril, gently enveloping the creature's injured limb. "*Its pain is immense,*" it said. "*But it can be healed.*"

The Doctor watched as Venom's tendrils pulsed with a soft, healing energy, mending the creature's wounds. The small being chirped softly, its light growing brighter as it fluttered its wings.

"There," the Doctor said with a smile. "Good as new."

The other creatures surrounded them, their lights pulsing in unison as if in gratitude. The Doctor stood, his hearts swelling with pride. "See, Venom? This is what we're meant to do. Not just to save worlds, but to bring hope."

"*Hope is a powerful force,*" Venom said. "*More powerful than I ever understood.*"

As they returned to the TARDIS, the Doctor leaned against the console, his hands brushing the familiar controls. "So, what do you think, Venom? A Time Lord and a symbiote, roaming the universe together. Has a nice ring to it, doesn't it?"

"*It is... fitting,*" Venom replied. "*We are stronger together than we ever were apart.*"

The Doctor's smile widened. "That's the spirit."

He pulled a lever, and the TARDIS shuddered as it began to dematerialize. The sound of its engines echoed through the console room, a sound that carried with it the promise of endless possibilities.

"Right then," the Doctor said, his voice brimming with excitement. "Let's see what's out there."

"*Together,*" Venom said.

The TARDIS vanished into the Time Vortex, its light leaving the small, glowing planet behind. The universe, forever changed by the bond between the Doctor and Venom, awaited their next adventure.

And for the first time in a long time, the Doctor felt whole—not as a Time Lord, not as a solitary traveler, but as something entirely new. Together, they were more than a force for good.

They were Venom Eternal.

Appendix

The History of the Symbiotes and Their Connection to the Time Lords

The symbiotes, also known as the Klyntar, are an ancient, sentient species that originated on their eponymous homeworld. They evolved as a collective of organic life forms capable of bonding with other species to enhance survival, often referred to as *symbiosis*. Over the millennia, this ability grew into both a blessing and a curse, depending on their intent and the will of their host.

Origins

The Klyntar developed as a species seeking harmony. Initially, their bonds were formed with the intention of mutual benefit, allowing them to thrive on Klyntar's challenging terrain. However, a schism arose within their kind—some symbiotes saw the bonds as partnerships, while others saw them as tools for dominance. This divide eventually gave rise to the hive mind, a controlling psychic force that united the aggressive faction under a singular, oppressive goal: universal domination.

The hive's influence spread across galaxies, leading to the enslavement of countless species. Over time, their reputation as parasites overshadowed their origins as protectors. Despite this, remnants of the symbiotes who resisted the hive continued to exist, scattered and hidden, seeking to escape their dark legacy.

The Time Lords and the Symbiotes

Millennia before the Doctor's encounter with Venom, the Time Lords became aware of the symbiotes during their exploration of the greater universe. Some records suggest that early Time Lords sought to weaponize the symbiotes' bonding abilities, experimenting with their psychic connections to enhance Gallifreyan technologies.

The experiments were ultimately deemed too dangerous, as the hive's influence threatened to infiltrate even the Time Lords' advanced defenses. The experiments were abandoned, and the symbiotes were classified as a universal threat. These records were buried deep within the Matrix, left untouched until the Doctor's bond with Venom unearthed their forgotten history.

The Doctor and Venom's alliance marked the first time a Time Lord successfully coexisted with a symbiote without succumbing to the hive. Their partnership became a symbol of the potential for redemption, breaking the cycle of fear and mistrust between the symbiotes and the rest of the universe.

Glossary of Symbiote-Related Terms and Characters

Symbiote (Klyntar):

A sentient, amorphous organism capable of bonding with a host to enhance physical and mental capabilities. Symbiotes vary greatly in temperament and purpose, ranging from protective partners to destructive parasites.

The Hive Mind:

A psychic network that once controlled the aggressive faction of symbiotes, driving their quest for universal domination. Destroyed through the combined efforts of the Doctor and Venom.

Host:

A being bonded to a symbiote. The nature of the bond depends on the symbiote's intent and the host's compatibility. A mutual bond enhances both, while a parasitic bond drains the host.

Venom:

The symbiote bonded to the Doctor, originally part of the hive but ultimately choosing freedom. Venom evolved into an independent being, capable of deep thought and moral reasoning through its connection with the Doctor.

Klyntar Homeworld:

The symbiotes' planet, a living ecosystem where organic and symbiotic life forms coexist. Following the destruction of the hive, it became a hub for rebuilding and redefining symbiote culture.

The Core:

The psychic nexus that maintained the hive's control over symbiotes across the universe. Its destruction by the Doctor and Venom liberated the symbiotes.

Symbiotic Nexus:
A concept introduced by the Doctor, referring to the potential for symbiotes and other species to coexist peacefully as equals.

Vareshka Prime:
A planet where symbiotes and their hosts coexist in harmony, offering a model for mutualistic symbiosis.

The Custodian of the Matrix:
An ancient AI within the Time Lords' Matrix that revealed the hidden history of Gallifrey's interaction with the symbiotes.

Behind-the-Scenes Insights into the Doctor and Venom's Fusion

The Bonding Process:
The bond between the Doctor and Venom was forged under extreme circumstances. When the Doctor encountered Venom on Klyntar, it was a matter of survival for both. The bond began as a pragmatic alliance, but over time, it deepened into something unprecedented—a true partnership. Venom absorbed traces of the Doctor's regeneration energy, which allowed it to evolve and develop a moral compass, while the Doctor gained physical enhancements and an expanded sense of perception.

Challenges of Coexistence:
The fusion was not without its struggles. The Doctor often wrestled with the idea of losing his individuality, while Venom grappled with its instinctual tendencies toward dominance. These conflicts, while difficult, ultimately strengthened their bond, teaching them the value of balance and trust.

The Symbiotic Identity:

Over time, the Doctor and Venom achieved a state of perfect symbiosis, where their thoughts and abilities aligned seamlessly. This fusion allowed them to confront challenges in ways neither could alone, combining the Doctor's ingenuity and Venom's raw power. Their unified identity became a force for good, proving that even the most unlikely alliances could change the universe.

The Impact on the Universe:

The Doctor and Venom's partnership inspired both awe and fear across the cosmos. They became a symbol of redemption for the symbiotes and a challenge to the status quo for the Time Lords. Through their actions, they redefined the narrative of what symbiotes could be—partners, not parasites.

Unanswered Questions:

Though the Doctor and Venom have embraced their bond, questions remain about its permanence. Can they ever truly separate, and would they even want to? The answers lie in the future, as they continue to navigate their shared existence.

The Future Awaits:

The Doctor and Venom's journey has just begun. Their bond has changed them both, and the universe itself is forever altered by their actions. As they step into the unknown, they carry with them the promise of hope, redemption, and endless possibilities. Together, they are more than Time Lord and symbiote.

They are Venom Eternal.

Message from the Author:

I hope you enjoyed this book, I love astrology and knew there was not a book such as this out on the shelf. I love metaphysical items as well. Please check out my other books:

-Life of Government Benefits

-My life of Hell

-My life with Hydrocephalus

-Red Sky

-World Domination:Woman's rule

-World Domination:Woman's Rule 2: The War

-Life and Banishment of Apophis: book 1

-The Kidney Friendly Diet

-The Ultimate Hemp Cookbook

-Creating a Dispensary(legally)

-Cleanliness throughout life: the importance of showering from childhood to adulthood.

-Strong Roots: The Risks of Overcoddling children

-Hemp Horoscopes: Cosmic Insights and Earthly Healing

- Celestial Hemp Navigating the Zodiac: Through the Green Cosmos

-Astrological Hemp: Aligning The Stars with Earth's Ancient Herb

-The Astrological Guide to Hemp: Stars, Signs, and Sacred Leaves

-Green Growth: Innovative Marketing Strategies for your Hemp Products and Dispensary

-Cosmic Cannabis

-Astrological Munchies

-Henry The Hemp

-Zodiacal Roots: The Astrological Soul Of Hemp

- Green Constellations: Intersection of Hemp and Zodiac

-Hemp in The Houses: An astrological Adventure Through The Cannabis Galaxy

-Galactic Ganja Guide

Heavenly Hemp

Zodiac Leaves

Doctor Who Astrology

Cannastrology

Stellar Satvias and Cosmic Indicas

Celestial Cannabis: A Zodiac Journey

AstroHerbology: The Sky and The Soil: Volume 1

AstroHerbology:Celestial Cannabis:Volume 2

Cosmic Cannabis Cultivation

The Starry Guide to Herbal Harmony: Volume 1

The Starry Guide to Herbal Harmony: Cannabis Universe: Volume 2

Yugioh Astrology: Astrological Guide to Deck, Duels and more

Nightmare Mansion: Echoes of The Abyss

Nightmare Mansion 2: Legacy of Shadows

Nightmare Mansion 3: Shadows of the Forgotten

Nightmare Mansion 4: Echoes of the Damned

The Life and Banishment of Apophis: Book 2

Nightmare Mansion: Halls of Despair

Healing with Herb: Cannabis and Hydrocephalus

Planetary Pot: Aligning with Astrological Herbs: Volume 1

Fast Track to Freedom: 30 Days to Financial Independence Using AI, Assets, and Agile Hustles

Cosmic Hemp Pathways

How to Become Financially Free in 30 Days: 10,000 Paths to Prosperity

Zodiacal Herbage: Astrological Insights: Volume 1

Nightmare Mansion: Whispers in the Walls

The Daleks Invade Atlantis

Henry the hemp and Hydrocephalus

10X The Kidney Friendly Diet

Cannabis Universe: Adult coloring book

Hemp Astrology: The Healing Power of the Stars

Zodiacal Herbage: Astrological Insights: Cannabis Universe: Volume 2

Planetary Pot: Aligning with Astrological Herbs: Cannabis Universes: Volume 2

Doctor Who Meets the Replicators and SG-1: The Ultimate Battle for Survival

Nightmare Mansion: Curse of the Blood Moon

The Celestial Stoner: A Guide to the Zodiac

Cosmic Pleasures: Sex Toy Astrology for Every Sign

Hydrocephalus Astrology: Navigating the Stars and Healing Waters

Lapis and the Mischievous Chocolate Bar

Celestial Positions: Sexual Astrology for Every Sign

Apophis's Shadow Work Journal: : A Journey of Self-Discovery and Healing

Kinky Cosmos: Sexual Kink Astrology for Every Sign

Digital Cosmos: The Astrological Digimon Compendium

Stellar Seeds: The Cosmic Guide to Growing with Astrology

Apophis's Daily Gratitude Journal

Cat Astrology: Feline Mysteries of the Cosmos

The Cosmic Kama Sutra: An Astrological Guide to Sexual Positions

Unleash Your Potential: A Guided Journal Powered by AI Insights

Whispers of the Enchanted Grove

Cosmic Pleasures: An Astrological Guide to Sexual Kinks

369, 12 Manifestation Journal

Whisper of the nocturne journal(blank journal for writing or drawing)

The Boogey Book

Locked In Reflection: A Chastity Journey Through Locktober

Generating Wealth Quickly:

How to Generate $100,000 in 24 Hours

Star Magic: Harness the Power of the Universe

The Flatulence Chronicles: A Fart Journal for Self-Discovery

The Doctor and The Death Moth

Seize the Day: A Personal Seizure Tracking Journal

The Ultimate Boogeyman Safari: A Journey into the Boogie World and Beyond

Whispers of Samhain: 1,000 Spells of Love, Luck, and Lunar Magic: Samhain Spell Book

Apophis's guides:

Witch's Spellbook Crafting Guide for Halloween

<u>Frost & Flame: The Enchanted Yule Grimoire of 1000 Winter Spells</u>

<u>The Ultimate Boogey Goo Guide & Spooky Activities for Halloween Fun</u>

Harmony of the Scales: A Libra's Spellcraft for Balance and Beauty

The Enchanted Advent: 36 Days of Christmas Wonders

Nightmare Mansion: The Labyrinth of Screams

Harvest of Enchantment: 1,000 Spells of Gratitude, Love, and Fortune for Thanksgiving

The Boogey Chronicles: A Journal of Nightly Encounters and Shadowy Secrets

The 12 Days of Financial Freedom: A Step-by-Step Christmas Countdown to Transform Your Finances

Sigil of the Eternal Spiral Blank Journal

A Christmas Feast: Timeless Recipes for Every Meal

Holiday Stress-Free Solutions: A Survival Guide to Thriving During the Festive Season

Yu-Gi-Oh! Holiday Gifting Mastery: The Ultimate Guide for Fans and Newcomers Alike

Holiday Harmony: A Hydrocephalus Survival Guide for the Festive Season

Celestial Craft: The Witch's Almanac for 2025 – A Cosmic Guide to Manifestations, Moons, and Mystical Events

Doctor Who: The Toymaker's Winter Wonderland

Tulsa King Unveiled: A Thrilling Guide to Stallone's Mafia Masterpiece

Pendulum Craft: A Complete Guide to Crafting and Using Personalized Divination Tools

Nightmare Mansion: Santa's Eternal Eve

Starlight Noel: A Cosmic Journey through Christmas Mysteries

The Dark Architect: Unlocking the Blueprint of Existence

Surviving the Embrace: The Ultimate Guide to Encounters with The Hugging Molly

The Enchanted Codex: Secrets of the Craft for Witches, Wiccans, and Pagans

Harvest of Gratitude: A Complete Thanksgiving Guide

Yuletide Essentials: A Complete Guide to an Authentic and Magical Christmas

Celestial Smokes: A Cosmic Guide to Cigars and Astrology

Living in Balance: A Comprehensive Survival Guide to Thriving with Diabetes Insipidus

Cosmic Symbiosis: The Venom Zodiac Chronicles

The Cursed Paw of Ambition

Cosmic Symbiosis: The Astrological Venom Journal

Celestial Wonders Unfold: A Stargazer's Guide to the Cosmos (2024-2029)

The Ultimate Black Friday Prepper's Guide: Mastering Shopping Strategies and Savings

Cosmic Sales: The Astrological Guide to Black Friday Shopping
Legends of the Corn Mother and Other Harvest Myths
Whispers of the Harvest: The Corn Mother's Journal
The Evergreen Spellbook
The Doctor Meets the Boogeyman
The White Witch of Rose Hall's SpellBook
The Gingerbread Golem's Shadow: A Study in Sweet Darkness
The Gingerbread Golem Codex: An Academic Exploration of Sweet Myths
The Gingerbread Golem Grimoire: Sweet Magicks and Spells for the Festive Witch
The Curse of the Gingerbread Golem
10-minute Christmas Crafts for kids
<u>Christmas Crisis Solutions: The Ultimate Last-Minute Survival Guide</u>
Gingerbread Golem Recipes: Holiday Treats with a Magical Twist
The Infinite Key: Unlocking Mystical Secrets of the Ages
Enchanted Yule: A Wiccan and Pagan Guide to a Magical and Memorable Season
Dinosaurs of Power: Unlocking Ancient Magick
Astro-Dinos: The Cosmic Guide to Prehistoric Wisdom
Gallifrey's Yule Logs: A Festive Doctor Who Cookbook
The Dino Grimoire: Secrets of Prehistoric Magick
The Gift They Never Knew They Needed
The Gingerbread Golem's Culinary Alchemy: Enchanting Recipes for a Sweetly Dark Feast
A Time Lord Christmas: Holiday Adventures with the Doctor
Krampusproofing Your Home: Defensive Strategies for Yule
Silent Frights: A Collection of Christmas Creepypastas to Chill Your Bones
Santa Raptor's Jolly Carnage: A Dino-Claus Christmas Tale
Prehistoric Palettes: A Dino Wicca Coloring Journey
The Christmas Wishkeeper Chronicles

The Starlight Sleigh: A Holiday Journey
Elf Secrets: The True Magic of the North Pole
Candy Cane Conjurations
Cooking with Kids: Recipes Under 20 Minutes
Doctor Who: The TARDIS Confiscation
The Anxiety First Aid Kit: Quick Tools to Calm Your Mind
Frosty Whispers: A Winter's Tale
The Infinite Key: Unlocking the Secrets to Prosperity, Resilience, and Purpose
The Grasping Void: Why You'll Regret This Purchase
Astrology for Busy Bees: Star Signs Simplified
The Instant Focus Formula: Cut Through the Noise
The Secret Language of Colors: Unlocking the Emotional Codes
Sacred Fossil Chronicles: Blank Journal
The Christmas Cottage Miracle
Feeding Frenzy: Graboid-Inspired Recipes
Manifest in Minutes: The Quick Law of Attraction Guide

If you want solar for your home go here: https://www.harborsolar.live/apophisenterprises/

Get Some Tarot cards: https://www.makeplayingcards.com/sell/ apophis-occult-shop

Get some shirts: https://www.bonfire.com/store/apophis-shirt-emporium/

<u>**Instagrams:**</u>
@apophis_enterprises,
@apophisbookemporium,
@apophisscardshop
Twitter: @apophisenterpr1
Tiktok:@apophisenterprise
Youtube: @sg1fan23477, @FiresideRetreatKingdom
Hive: @sg1fan23477
CheeLee: @SG1fan23477

Podcast: Apophis Chat Zone: https://open.spotify.com/show/5zXbrCLEV2xzCp8ybrfHsk?si=fb4d4fdbdce44dec

Newsletter: https://apophiss-newsletter-27c897.beehiiv.com/

If you want to support me or see posts of other projects that I have come over to: **buymeacoffee.com/mpetchinskg**
I post there daily several times a day

Get your Dinowicca or Christmas themed digital products, especially Santa Raptor songs and other musics. Here: **https://sg1fan23477.gumroad.com**

Apophis Yuletide Digital has not only digital Christmas items, but it will have all things with Dinowicca as well as other Digital products.